Ecosystems Matter

Ecosystems Matter

Jessica Jane Robinson

Resilience Birthright Productions

ISBN: 978-0-9997226-2-6 (Paperback)

Library of Congress Control Number: 1-15105966181

Any reference to historical events, real people, or real places is used fictitiously. Names, characters, and places are products of the author's imagination.

Front cover image by Cato Creations LLC.
Illustrations by Cato Creations LLC.
Book design by Jessica Jane Robinson.

Printed by Resilience Birthright Productions, in the United States of America.

First printing edition 2026.

Resilience Birthright
PO Box 6115
Alameda,CA, 94501

www.RBRORG.com

In loving memory of my grandmother,
Juanita Blair —
who encouraged me to follow my dreams,
who believed in me before the world did,
my first executive producer
and forever my number one fan.

Her love continues to guide my steps,
and I am endlessly grateful.

This book is also dedicated to all the Earth Warrior children —
young and old —
may you stay empowered, inspired,
and grow boldly in your God-given talents
as you help heal our planet.

Introduction

Once upon a time, a little girl with a huge heart and love for nature lived on a small island in the Pacific Bay—the Bay Area, to be exact. Her family and her friends at school called her Jessica.

Jessica has always been a unique little girl. She was born with gifts that made her sensitive and aware of all life around her, more than most children and adults. As a baby, she made rare friendships with an apple tree she called Terry the Apple Tree, a monarch butterfly called Beau the Butterfly, a honey bee called Bumbles the Bee, a gray squirrel called Sunny the Squirrel, and two earthworms she called Mr. and Mrs. Wiggles the Worms. She loved spending time with her friends in her grandmother's backyard. They had the most interesting conversations, and Jessica learned a lot about nature and the ways of the natural world from listening to her friends share their stories on how they help the planet and about the cycles of nature.

Terry, Beau, Bumbles, Sunny, and Mr. and Mrs. Wiggles called Jessica Baby **Resilience** because they knew that Jessica was without her mom and dad, yet she was **resilient**. They knew Jessica was entirely from another world; she was not an earthling but from another planet thirteen galaxies away (but that's another story for another day). They could see how special Jessica was and how she always kept a smile on her face even though they knew she carried so much sadness from not knowing where her real mom and dad were. Jessica was found by earthlings—humans—who took her in and raised her as their own. The friends could see Jessica was grateful for her human grandmother, who raised her as her grandchild. Jessica was strong and brave and showed she could overcome many obstacles, so they called her Baby Resilience, or Baby Res for short. Baby Res displayed a sense of resilience as she faced life, determined to be a positive light and inspire other humans to love the planet and the natural world and have a love for her dear friends as she did.

As we dive deeper into Baby Res and her friends' story, we will learn about the **interconnectedness** of life on our planet. Baby Res and her friends believe that understanding and appreciating the cycles of nature can lead to a profound respect and love for our world, inspiring us to protect the earth and all life on it.

Resilient (adjective)

1. (of a person or animal) able to withstand or recover quickly from difficult conditions.

2. (of a substance or object) able to recoil or spring back into shape after bending, stretching, or being compressed.

Resilience refers to the ability to successfully adapt to stressors, maintaining psychological well-being in the face of adversity.

Resilience is having the ability to "bounce back" from difficult experiences.

Interconnectedness (noun)

  • the state of having different parts or things connected or related to each other:

  • the way in which people, nature, and objects interact with one another to form a complex whole.

Interconnectedness for future generations means understanding that creating a better world requires awareness, respect, and collaboration with both nature and humanity, ensuring the sustainability of our environment and biodiversity.

Prologue

A few years had gone by since Jessica started school. She loved learning and exploring exciting topics, reading, writing, and solving math problems. Learning was an activity that Jessica loved with her whole heart, besides spending time with her grandmother, close relatives, and her special friends in the backyard, Terry, Sunny, Beau, Bumbles, and Mr. and Mrs. Wiggles. But what truly set Jessica apart was her unique bond with nature. She was often seen talking to trees, plants, animals, and bugs, and her enthusiasm for her nature friends was unmatched. Unfortunately, most of the children didn't understand this bond and chose to avoid Jessica, thinking she was weird and strange.

As Jessica grew older, she decided to keep her fascination with her animal, insect, and plant friends a secret that only she, her grandmother, and her friends in the backyard knew about. Jessica's grandmother called her backyard friends imaginary, and she would always say that she saw nothing wrong with having an imagination. In fact, Jessica's grandmother encouraged her to imagine, create, write, and share stories because she thought one day Jessica might write an award-winning book, play, or something great.

However, to feel comfortable around other children her age, Jessica learned to keep her special friends a secret. So they remained a secret and a joy once she arrived home from school. Jessica learned to enjoy sharing stories of what she learned during her studies and was eager to hear what her friends would share, which only deepened Jessica's knowledge and understanding of the planet she called home.

COMPOST

CHAPTER ONE:
School of Ecosystems

It was Friday. Jessica had just finished the first week of school, and she's feeling mixed emotions about her experience. She walks into the living room of her grandmother, Charlotte, and is greeted by the family dog named Bear. Jessica bends down to pick Bear up and gives him a kiss on his head and a hug. She puts him down and begins think about what to share with her grandmother first. Should she start with the positive news about her excitement learning about ecosystems within environments in class or about how she was struggling to make friendships with other students? Just as Jessica was weighing out what to say, her grandmother was the first to speak. "How's your day, Jessica? What did you learn today? Any luck making new friends?" Charlotte smiles, giving Jessica a big hug as she rose from the couch.

Jessica breaks into tears of sadness. "No, no new friends today, Grandma. I was too nervous, and talking to the other kids was hard."

With concern in her eyes, Grandma asks, "Why were you nervous? I am sure the others feel similarly making new friends during the first week of school. You're a good girl, a sweet person, and smart. You just need to believe in yourself a little more. Be brave."

Jessica, looking down at the carpet, is a little embarrassed to admit, "But Grandma, I don't know how to start a conversation. I feel weird and don't know what to say."

Charlotte smiles, wipes a tear from Jessica's cheek, and says, "It's simple. Just start with a smile and say hi. You have a beautiful smile, and it's warm and welcoming. Start with a simple, friendly hello."

Jessica begins feeling relief that she is back home with Grandma and her friends in the backyard. "Okay, I will try that next week on Monday." Jessica gives her grandmother one last hug before she begins to rush to the back door that leads to the yard.

Charlotte's voice trails behind Jessica, "You didn't share what you learned today!"

Jessica stops by the back door, turns back toward her grandmother, and responds with excitement, "I learned about ecosystems and environments today!"

Charlotte approaches her at the back door as she gathers laundry from the laundry room. She begins folding the clothes and continues her regular interest in her granddaughter's learning. "What did you learn about ecosystems and environments? Can you share something you remember?"

Jessica takes a moment to gather her thoughts. "**Ecosystems** are where living things (organisms) and nonliving things interact in a physical environment in a specific place. Our **environment** is everything around us: our earth, sun, atmosphere, climate, weather, and land."

Grandma lifts her head after finishing folding a towel. She looks at Jessica standing in the back doorway and asks, "Do you know what that means, 'where living and nonliving things interact?' Do you have any examples to share with me?"

Jessica nods and says proudly, "Yes, as a matter of fact, our home is our environment and ecosystem. We live in our home, and we're alive; we have our little dog, Bear, and the plants inside the house are alive too." Jessica points to the washroom sink. "We have water that we use for bathing, drinking, and cooking, and water is nonliving, and it supports life inside the house." Jessica's hand points to the plant on the windowsill. "The soil in the potted plant contains nutrients and tiny organisms that help the plants grow just like outside. The sunlight that goes through the windows every day supports the plant in growing. The sunlight is nonliving, and it gives living things like plants energy. And Bear loves to lie out in the sunspots during the day; the sunlight supports him, too!"

Jessica grabs her grandmother's hand and leads her into the kitchen, pointing to the refrigerator. "Grandma, even the food we eat was once living, too, plants and animals, and they provide nourishment for our family. All the interactions within our home make an ecosystem."

Charlotte smiles at Jessica, and with encouragement in her

eyes, she says, "Yes, do you have any more examples?"

Jessica beams confidently and raises her arms towards the ceiling as if trying to grasp the stars in the sky, looking up. "Even the air we breathe—it's nonliving, but so important for all life on this planet and inside our home. The plants in the house take in the carbon dioxide that we exhale and release oxygen. That is a really good example of living and nonliving interacting together inside our home."

Jessica looks at the recycling bin. "We separate our waste, we recycle as much as we can at home, and the nonliving materials, like our cardboard, metal cans, glass bottles, and plastic containers, can be recycled and reused again. That's how we help our planet, the ecosystem, and environment outside our home."

Charlotte smiles at Jessica, giving her a big hug and kiss on her forehead. "You're such an intelligent little girl. Keep up the good work. I am proud of you, my dear."

Jessica grins, looks around the kitchen, and points to the compost bin. "Even the **compost** bin has bacteria that we can't see that are living, and they help break down the food. Bacteria are similar to decomposers outside."

Grandma looks at Jessica with curiosity. "Decomposers?"

"Yes, Grandma, decomposers are a part of matter within an ecosystem. **Matter** is made up of living and nonliving things within an ecosystem. We all have roles in our ecosystem, kind of like a superhero team. The superhero team is made of **matter, decomposers, producers,** and **consumers,** and they all have roles to play when taking care of the planet and keeping it in balance," Jessica explains matter-of-factly.

"Well, sweetheart, keep up the good work. Why don't you go outside and get the last bit of sun before dinner? While you're at it, I would love to hear of any more examples you come up with about the superhero team that is outside in the garden. The garden is another ecosystem full of mysteries to discover. You can tell us all about what you find at dinnertime." Grandma gently motions Jessica to the back door while she walks back to her laundry that she was folding.

"I want to share what I learned with Terry and see what she says about the topic. I will report back to you in a little bit, Grandma." Jessica beams with excitement in her voice.

Jessica's grandmother grins. "Okay, I look forward to what imaginary Terry will share with you. Enjoy your time outside. Dinner will be ready in two hours."

Jessica nods her head and runs outside into her grandmother's garden, which Jessica and her nature friends know as "Grandma's Secret Garden."

CHAPTER TWO

Grandma's Secret Ecosystem

Charlotte's garden got its name, Grandma's Secret Garden, because it reminds Jessica of her favorite books, The Secret Garden by Frances Hodgson Burnett and The Chronicles of Narnia by C.S. Lewis. Grandma's Secret Garden is full of flowers and smells of blooming roses and California fuchsias in the spring, summer, fall, and early winter. The garden has vegetables that her grandmother plants seasonally, with an apple tree, a big oak tree with a treehouse and a hummingbird feeder on one of the branches, a bird bath, and a little white metal garden bench that looks like it belongs in a fairy forest. Grandma's Secret Garden reminds Jessica of the magical land of Narnia because of her nature friends, who would come to life and talk to her, and because it is where she is no longer a little girl who doesn't fit in, but a superhero they call "Resilience," or "Res" for short.

"Hello, Baby Res." The greeting is coming from the smiling apple tree. "Um, I mean Res. You're growing into a fine young lady, and I must remember that we are calling you Res now.

You're not a baby anymore."

Res runs to her friend Terry the Apple Tree and gives the tree the biggest hug. "I am so happy to see you, Terry! I finished my first week of school."

Terry smiles at Res, and one of her branches waves in the wind as it motions Res to sit under the shade of her tree branches. "How did it go? You're in the first week of school?"

Res's smile fades, and a tear drops from her eye. "Not well at all. I was too afraid to make friends. I'm too different."

Terry looks at her friend and gently reminds Res she is loved. "Res, you are different from all the friends in Grandma's Secret Garden, and that doesn't stop us from being your friends and loving you for who you are. I am confident that you will find your true friends. Just put on your superhero cape next week, be brave, and smile."

"That's what Grandma said too—to be brave and smile." Res shrugs and decides to change the subject. "You know what, Terry?! I am learning about ecosystems and matter, living and nonliving, and I have the assignment to investigate examples of matter, decomposers, producers, and consumers in this garden and this world."

Terry smiles and says excitedly, "Ahh, I see. The planet has many different types of ecosystems and bodies of water."

Res looks at Terry and asks, "Terry, would you consider landscapes or even the earth living or nonliving?"

There is a moment of silence as the wind gently blows her branches, and a leaf slowly flutters to the grass next to Res. They both look at the leaf, and then Terry answers softly, "I would say both, my dear; the earth and landscapes combine living and nonliving. On land, there are physical features—for example, mountains, soil, rocks, and rivers—which are nonliving. At the same time, landscapes can include trees, plants, animals, soil, and microorganisms, and they are all indeed living."

Res's eyes light up as another ah-ha moment comes to her mind. "Terry, Grandma took me to Lake Tahoe and Yosemite this past summer. Both landscapes have a mixture of living and nonliving. The nonliving are the mountains, rocks, rivers, and lakes that create the land that the living matter—like soil, plants, and animals—interacts with and depends on, creating the ecosystem."

Terry continues, "Yes, Lake Tahoe, Yosemite, the Redwoods, the Amazon, and the entire planet are environments and have living things that play their parts in their delicate ecosystems."

Res adds, "Like the superhero team of **matter, decomposers, producers,** and **consumers** I was talking about with Grandma."

Terry smiles once more. "The nonliving matter that doesn't breathe or grow, like mountains, rocks, rivers, and lakes, is very important because it gives animals and plants a place to live and find food. Both living and nonliving matter work hand in hand to create the beautiful world we call home."

Res looks at Terry and then around Grandma's Secret Garden. "Terry, Grandma gave me an assignment. She wants me to share how her garden is an ecosystem for you and all my friends here."

Just then, Sunny the Squirrel scurries down the tree, having awakened from his nap. Beau the Butterfly and Bumbles the Bee overhear the conversation as they are visiting Grandma's blooming roses as usual. Mr. and Mrs. Wiggles pop up from the vegetable garden to join in the conversation.

Res is extremely excited to see all her beloved friends.

Just then, a hummingbird zips through the garden and hovers by Res's head. "Hi, I overheard you have an assignment to share how this garden is an ecosystem. I am Flora the Hummingbird, at your service, and it would be an honor to share what this garden has meant to me these past few weeks."

All the friends, including Res, introduce themselves to their new friend Flora. Glad to be accepted into the community of friends, Flora begins to share her insight. "Grandma's Secret Garden is a paradise for me. The plants give me food, the birdbath gives me water, Terry the Apple Tree and the oak tree give me places to rest and shelter from wind and rain."

Res claps her hands, excited to hear more.

"I love your grandmother's flowers; her roses smell nice, but the California fuchsias are my favorite. The fuchsia is filled with nectar, and the flower's tubular shape is perfect for my beak. I carry pollen all around with me, and I help the flowers to grow new seeds. I don't mind sharing the flowers with Beau the Butterfly or Bumbles the Bee because we all have our roles. The hummingbird feeder gives me another source of nectar and boosts my energy when I must migrate north. The garden is becoming my little kingdom, and I love how everyone works together and keeps the garden beautiful."

All the friends in the garden smile at Flora and then take a moment to admire the garden they all cherish.

After a peaceful silence, Sunny the Squirrel chimes in, "Uh hum, may I share what Grandma's Secret Garden means to me?"

Res looks at her squirrel friend and nods. "Yes, Sunny. I would love your assistance. Everyone's point of view is welcome."

"Grandma's Secret Garden is my home as well. Terry the Apple Tree and the oak tree and tree house are the center of my world. I love to nibble on Terry's apples, and the oak tree gives me acorns that give me nutrients and energy during the fall and winter. Both tree branches are perfect for climbing and keeping me safe, and I have a great view of the garden. I also like to hide in the treehouse, rest, and store some of my food there. The air is always fresh and smells of yummy fruit and flowers. The birdbath is a wonderful place for me to find fresh water, especially on hot days. Grandma's seasonal vegetables are wonderful snacks, and I enjoy the leftover seeds they bring. I spend most of my time gathering food, like Terry's apples, seeds from the garden and neighboring yards, and, on occasion, some vegetables from the garden. I love how rich the soil is in the garden. I dig in the soil and bury my food for later, and I end up helping Grandma plant more seeds. More often than not, I forget where I buried some seeds, and they sprout sometimes by mistake in the wrong places in the garden."

Res begins to laugh. Sunny stops speaking, and everyone

looks at Res, waiting for her to share what is so funny. Res is doing her best to get her words out through the laughter. "You're the culprit!" Res points at Sunny, laughing. "Grandma was so confused this summer about how some squash ended up growing with her fuchsias. It was you!"

Sunny confesses with a sheepish tone, "Yes, it was me. I love squash seeds, and I snacked on a few and took a couple to hide away for later. I forgot exactly where I stashed them. Grandma's soil is very rich in nutrition and healthy, and it is easy for seeds to sprout."

Everyone begins to laugh, including Sunny. With tears in her eyes from all the laughter, Res looks at her friends with gratitude. "Thank you, everyone. I am so happy that you are all my friends."

Just then, another voice surfaces from near the oak tree trunk, near the shrub of sage and blue elderberry aromas. A tiny mushroom, bright red with white spots looking like an umbrella, stood proudly next to the oak tree trunk. "Hello, my name is Anna Mycelium, the Amanita Muscaria. I couldn't help but hear the wonderful discussion about this magical garden I call my home. As a matter of fact, I take pride in helping Grandma's Secret Garden's soil become so rich."

Res had never noticed this new member of the garden before and begins to approach Anna Mycelium with curiosity. She is just about to touch Anna Mycelium's red-and-white spotted, umbrella-like top when Anna Mycelium's voice stops her hand in mid-motion.

Anna Mycelium's voice is friendly yet very stern, with a conviction that could not be ignored or denied. "I understand my appearance brings curiosity and intrigue. However, please do not touch me. I am not for eating, and I am actually quite poisonous, but I play an important role in Grandma's Secret Garden. Would you mind if I share my contribution to the ecosystem we have here?"

Everyone simultaneously says with huge delight, "Yes, please."

Res walks over to the white fairy bench near the oak tree and sits down. She is eager to learn more about the mysteries in the garden.

Anna Mycelium begins her story. "Some refer to me as the queen of the forest floor because I am not an ordinary mushroom. In fact, I have a vital role to play in the environment. I am responsible for spreading an underground network of threads called mycelium. You can consider the **mycelium network** to be like the internet and communication lines within the soil, where the roots of the nearby plants—like the oak tree, Terry, the flowers, the shrubs, and the vegetables—and all different species mutually benefit from the ability to communicate and interact with each other. You can call it a **symbiotic relationship**. My mycelium network connects the roots of all the plants in the garden with the water and nutrients they all need. I prefer to live in cool, damp, shady, moist soil, so being beneath the big oak tree is perfect. One of my favorite jobs is breaking down fallen leaves, twigs, and other dying plants and turning all the material into rich, dark soil. The dark soil I create helps the entire garden by recycling the nutrients and keeping the soil healthy."

Res's eyes widen with this new information. "Anna Mycelium, you mean you help make compost?"

Anna Mycelium responds cheerfully, "Yes, I do."

After another moment of silence, Mr. and Mrs. Wiggles speak together. "May we contribute to this story?"

Res turns to her friends, Mr. and Mrs. Wiggles, who had moved slowly toward the fairy bench near Res's feet.

Mrs. Wiggles looks to her husband. "Do you mind if I start first, my love?"

Mr. Wiggles nods, agreeing for his wife to start their part in the garden ecosystem story.

Mrs. Wiggles begins to speak with a kind and gentle voice. "Mr. Wiggles and I do a lot of digging and wiggling through the soil. We create tunnels that help water and air reach the roots of the plants in the garden; this is called **aeration**. The tunnels also make it easier for plant roots to grow deep and strong. We also help by eating what Anna Mycelium and other bacteria helped break down, such as dead leaves and plants in the garden. After we eat the plant and leaf decay, we digest and leave behind nutritious castings, also known as worm poop."

Terry joins in politely. "Mrs. Wiggles, if you don't mind, I'd like to share that your castings are a superfood for the soil that all the plants thrive on, including myself.

Mr. Wiggles adds, "As a matter of fact, Mrs. Wiggles and I are extremely grateful for Anna Mycelium's work. She breaks down the tougher materials, and Mrs. Wiggles and I finish the job, turning what remains into rich soil."

"Wow," Beau the Butterfly says as he flutters over toward Res. "I always knew we all made a great team, but I never thought much about how. This conversation has been very informative."

All the friends nod and once again enjoy each other's presence in the beautiful silence inside Grandma's Secret Garden.

CHAPTER THREE

Balance Matters in Energy Transfers

Res and her friends are still sharing a pleasant moment of silence, admiring their beloved magical garden. Charlotte's voice can be heard from the kitchen window, calling, "Jessica, dinner will be ready in 30 minutes."

Res has another ah-ha moment. "Thank you! I think I am getting a good understanding of how everyone plays an important role in the garden. I told my grandma that I would explain everyone's superhero roles. I think I understand how we all work together."

Res looks at all her friends and shares more about what she learned at school. "This week, my teacher taught us about **matter** and **energy transfer** in ecosystems. Ecosystems consist of matter: living and nonliving things. Living matter are plants, animals, and organisms. The nonliving are air, nutrients, and water. The **decomposers** break down animal and plant matter, recycling the nutrients back into the soil and releasing energy into heat. The **producers** are plants that use **photosynthesis** to create their own food, using water, **carbon dioxide** (CO_2: a colorless, odorless gas), and sunlight. These plants provide nutritious food and energy for the animals that eat them. And lastly, the **consumers** are animals that eat other living things for energy."

Bumbles the Bee buzzes over to Res's head, eager to help. "Res, do you mind if I share what I have gathered about matter and energy transfer and all of us as a team working together?"

Res looks over to her friend, buzzing in place a few feet from where she is sitting. "Of course, Bumbles—you haven't shared at all yet!"

Bumbles the Bee buzzes in a circle, excited to share her new understanding. "Our entire team is of living matter; we're the superhero team. Terry the Apple Tree, the oak tree, and the flowers are producers. Anna Mycelium, the Amanita Muscaria, Mr. and Mrs. Wiggles, and the earthworms are decomposers. Sunny the Squirrel, Beau the Butterfly, Res, and of course me—we are consumers!"

Beau the Butterfly flutters to Bumbles and joins in. "The nonliving is just as important and supports all the living matter—all of us! The nonliving matter is the air we breathe, the nutrients we get from our food, and the water."

Res claps her hands with joy. "Thank you so much, friends. I am ready to share the mysteries I have uncovered with all of you to my family during dinner tonight."

Res gets up from the bench, says one last goodbye and goodnight to her nature friends, and heads back into the house. As soon as she enters her home, she immediately goes to the kitchen sink to wash her hands for dinner and then heads over to the dining room to join her grandma and Grace, the woman who found her as a baby.

Both women look adoringly at their Jessica and ask what she discovered in the backyard about the superhero team.

Jessica looks at both women and begins to share with a wide grin on her face. "Anna Mycelium—the Amanita Muscaria—and Mr. and Mrs. Wiggles are decomposers and break down dead and decomposing matter to help enrich the soil, and this helps them to nourish the trees and plants that are helping them grow. Anna Mycelium has a network in the soil called mycelium where the plants in the garden's roots can communicate what they need to succeed. Mr. and Mrs. Wiggles aerate the soil, making it easier for plants to grow their roots and absorb water and nutrients.

Terry the Apple Tree, the oak tree, and the flowers in the garden are all producers. They provide food, shelter, and oxygen to the ecosystem. Terry provides apples, and the oak tree provides acorns that Sunny the Squirrel enjoys eating. The flowers and shrubs provide nectar to Beau, Bumbles, and Flora.

Sunny the Squirrel, Beau the Butterfly, Bumbles the Bee, Flora the Hummingbird, and me—we're all consumers. Sunny helps plant seeds around the garden."

Jessica breaks into a little giggle. She looks at her grandmother, who seems a little confused about a random burst of giggling. Jessica does her best to regain her composure. She takes a deep breath and continues to share. "Beau the Butterfly, Bumbles the

Bee, and Flora the Hummingbird are all important. They help pollinate the garden while feeding on the flower nectar. And I am a living being, and I help care for the plants and animals in the garden; my role is to help maintain balance in the ecosystem."

Grandma takes a bite of her salad, chews for a few moments, swallows her food, and looks at her granddaughter with love and amazement. "Wow, that was wonderful. I am impressed with your discoveries from the garden."

"Yes, Grandma. I have one more thing to share because I have a vocabulary test this Monday, and I feel I understand the other scientific words better now. The conclusion of my discovery in the garden is the producers participate in an activity called **productivity**, where they make their own energy and food from the garden using sunlight, water, and nutrients from the soil to grow leaves, flowers, and fruits. The growth is called **biomass**, which is energy. The **energy flows** through the ecosystem from the plants to Sunny, Bumbles, Flora, and us, the consumers. The plants give energy in the forms of nectar, seeds, apples, and vegetables that we all need and get energy from. When plants and animals die, decomposers like Anna Mycelium, bacteria, and Mr. and Mrs. Wiggles break down the dead material, returning the nutrients to the soil and releasing the energy into the environment—this is called **decomposition**. The returned nutrients help the new plants grow in soil, and the cycle starts all over again. This is the complete **nutrient cycling** process that helps our ecosystem stay balanced."

Grandma puts her fork down on her plate and looks at Jessica with admiration. "You just keep on surprising me with all that you share and how quickly you learn. It's truly amazing!"

Grace joins the conversation. "Jess, how was school this week? Did you make any friends?"

Jessica drops her smile, and sadness takes over. "No, I did not. I don't know what to say."

"What do you mean you don't know what to say? You seem to have a lot to say to your imaginary friends in the garden. All that energy you put into your imagination should be directed toward making real friends. You're getting too old for imaginary friends; it's not healthy. I am not sure you should spend so much time in the backyard," Grace says with frustration.

Jessica's voice cracks with emotion as tears start to stream from her face. "I will try harder next week to make friends. I'm full. Is it okay if I go to bed early?"

Grandma steps in. "Yes, dear. You are excused."

Jessica gets up from the table and gives her grandma and Grace a hug goodnight. She grabs her dishes from the dining room table and brings them into the kitchen. Tears are still streaming from her eyes as she begins to wash them. Charlotte's voice interrupts her action. "Don't worry about the dishes, dear. I will take care of them."

Jessica nods and rushes to her room before her tears start to pour out, because she doesn't want her family to see how upset she has become.

Back in the dining room, Grandma looks at her daughter with questioning eyes. "Why did you have to be so hard on her?"

Grace snaps at her mother. "Hard on her?! When I was growing up, you would not have tolerated me having imaginary friends past kindergarten. You would have taken anything away that supported habits you considered bad. Jess is getting too old for this, and you are enabling her, and it's hurting her development. You're treating her differently than you did with me."

Charlotte looks at her daughter, not knowing what to say or how to defend Jessica without upsetting her further than she already is. Grandma chooses silence to avoid an argument with her daughter.

Jessica avoids talking about ecosystems and doesn't visit the garden that weekend to "maintain the peace" of the house.

CHAPTER FOUR:
Diverse Ecosystems

The weekend passes slowly, and Jessica does not visit her friends in Grandma's Secret Garden. There is tension in the house as Grace is still slightly angry with her mother for not raising Jessica with the same standards that she was held to. She is frustrated with Jessica because she does not understand why Jess is so different from how she was when she was Jessica's age. Jessica does her best not to add to the stress in the house as she finds herself moving around her home doing her weekend chores and studying quietly with her head down, not wanting to cause more upset. The end result of all the misunderstandings and resentment is a mostly silent house full of uncomfortable tension.

Finally, Monday has arrived. Jessica springs out of bed and is eager to get ready and head to school. This is unusual behavior for Jessica since school and the pressure to be in social settings with the other children cause her stress and anxiety. Still, this Monday, being anywhere is better than being trapped in her home where everyone is unhappy and barely communicating.

Once Jessica arrives in class, she is greeted by her teacher and given a pop quiz about ecosystems, matter, and energy flow. Jessica feels very confident about returning to school, since the questions in the quiz seem very simple and easy for her to answer after all the extra learning and examples she and her nature friends covered that last Friday.

After the quiz and the first part of the morning are over, Jessica's class is excused for recess. Recess and lunch have become the most disliked part of school for Jessica because she doesn't have any friends like the rest of her classmates. The children hang out in small groups, where some will sit near benches and trees or hang out on the blacktop playing games together until it is time to return to class. Jessica uses the break time to volunteer to help her teacher prep for the next lesson or help her school custodian clean up after lunch to avoid the awkwardness of not having anyone her age to talk to.

For this recess, Jessica decides to stick around after all her classmates go outside to play and asks her teacher if she can help out with anything. Ms. Olive, Jessica's teacher, is a kind woman. She is slender, with short brown hair, blue eyes, and a kind smile.

With compassion in her eyes, Ms. Olive points to the stack of books on the back table of the classroom. "Yes, you can help me put all the books and lesson plans at everyone's table." Ms. Olive is aware of Jessica's struggle to make friends with the other children. She doesn't want to encourage Jessica's avoidance toward socializing with other children, but at the same time, she believes Jessica will warm up to the right kids at the right time. Ms. Olive is very compassionate and plays along, pretending she doesn't realize that Jessica stays behind in order to avoid being alone outside. She allows Jessica to help her when there are things she can do in the classroom, like prepping for the following classroom lesson plans.

The recess bell rings and everyone returns to class. The students are greeted with books at their desks. The desks are organized by groups of three or four with the same number of students. Jessica is part of a group of only three students. Joelle and Ram are the two other students assigned to Jessica's table group. Both Ram and Joelle are both well-traveled students. Ram was born in India, and his parents are doctors who moved to the United States when he was three years old but traveled frequently to India and other parts of the world. Joelle's parents are professional researchers in cultures and languages from various parts of the world, and they run an import-export trading company for worldly goods.

As soon as all the students sit down, Ms. Olive begins the next lesson on ecosystems. "There are two types of ecosystems on our planet: **terrestrial ecosystems** and **aquatic ecosystems**. Does anyone know what terrestrial and aquatic mean?"

Joelle raises her hand. "Aquatic must mean water, like aquatic parks, where I can swim with dolphins."

Ms. Olive smiles at Joelle and looks at the rest of her class. "Yes, aquatic ecosystems are present in a body of water. Does anyone want to guess what terrestrial ecosystem means?"

One child's hand goes up immediately. Ms. Olive calls on him.

"Terrestrial? Oh, you mean extraterrestrial? So, does that mean aquatic is where the aliens go swimming? Do they paddleboard or just float around in UFOs?"

The whole class bursts into laughter, and Ms. Olive does her best to keep from laughing, too. "Very clever. Let's keep on topic."

Ram raises his hand. "Terrestrial means ecosystems that are on land?"

Ms. Olive quickly continues so she can keep the class's attention. "Yes, Ram. **Terrestrial ecosystems** are exclusively land-based ecosystems. There are four types: **forest, grassland, tundra, and desert**. I want you all to research the different climates and landscapes of these four terrestrial ecosystems by yourselves and, after fifteen minutes, brainstorm with each other about the types you have visited or lived in."

Ram, Joelle, and Jessica look at each other and then at their book of ecosystems and start to read. Jessica's attention and interest stay on forests. As a little girl, she always felt at home around trees. Terry the Apple Tree and the oak tree in Grandma's Secret Garden always welcome her with love, and she always feels at home when she visits national forest areas, such as Yosemite or the Redwoods. After fifteen minutes pass, Ms. Olive rings her bell as a signal for the class to switch from reading to discussing the different types of terrestrial ecosystems.

Ram offers to share first. "I was born in Jaipur, India, which is located in the state of Rajasthan. Rajasthan is very hot and dry, gets very little rain, and is home to the Thar Desert, also known as the Great Indian Desert. Jaipur is similar to a desert ecosystem. However, Jaipur is not deep in the desert and does get some rain. When my family and I traveled to the Taj Mahal in Agra, we drove past people with camels and cactus plants." Joelle and Jessica respectfully and quietly listen to Ram share his experience visiting India.

Once Ram finishes, Joelle volunteers to share her experiences. "My parents travel the world for work. When I was five, they took me to the tundra in Alaska. I remember the land being covered in snow and ice. There were no trees, just small shrubs. The air was very cold, and I could blow little clouds out of my mouth. I also saw a caribou with huge antlers when I was with my mother, who needed to take photos of nature in Alaska. One of my favorite memories is one night with my father as we watched the northern lights. When I was seven, my parents took me to the grasslands in East Africa. There are fields of tall grass everywhere and trees that look like giant bonsai trees, called acacia. The tundra is full of animals like zebras, elephants, giraffes, and even lions. All the animals live together and find enough food and water in the grasses and trees."

"Wow, that sounds so cool," Jessica says while listening to the stories. "I wish I could share stories of India, Alaska, or Africa. I have dreams of a land with trees, magical animals, and plants that seem out of this world. The only places that come close to the forest in my dreams are the Redwoods. When I visit the Redwoods with my family, it's like visiting a fairyland. Once, I walked through a tree with a tunnel carved out of it; it was like I stepped into a magical doorway into the forest. Some of the trees are thousands of years old. When I was with my grandma and Grace, I saw a tree with a trunk so big that even when we joined hands, we couldn't wrap around it. There are so many creatures, like owls, deer, and even banana slugs. I saw a banana slug on the trunk of a giant redwood tree; it was bright yellow!"

Just as Jessica finishes her story about seeing the banana slug, Ms. Olive rings her bell to get the class's attention and to have a few tables share their examples of the four terrestrial ecosystems.

After the last student shares their table's land-based ecosystem, Ms. Olive directs the class to the next exercise. "Now we are going to discuss **aquatic ecosystems**. There are two. Can anyone tell me what they are?"

Another student raises their hand to speak. "The two aquatic ecosystems are freshwater and saltwater."

Ms. Olive responds joyfully, "That's correct. However, the proper terms are **freshwater ecosystem** and **marine ecosystem**. Now, I would like you all to go back to your books and read about these two ecosystems, and in five minutes, share your experiences with these two types of aquatic ecosystems in your group."

Once again, the children in the class went back to reading their ecosystem textbook. After five minutes, Ms. Olive rings her bell once again to signal that it is time for the children to share stories with in their table groups.

This time, Jessica, feeling more comfortable speaking with Ram and Joelle, decides to go first. "My grandma takes me to visit Lake Tahoe and the Truckee River at least twice a year;

they're both freshwater ecosystems. This past summer, I got to go on a boat to see the lake. The lake was clear and cool to swim in. I jumped in and was cold at first, but then I started to feel fine and swam for a little bit. The lake is so beautiful; it has tall mountains and pine trees all around it. I also learned that Lake Tahoe is one of the biggest freshwater lakes in the world. Fish like trout and salmon live in the lake and are little creatures that help keep the water clean. The Truckee River is cool, too. I like how fast the river moves and the sound of the water rushing over the rocks. The river is important for the plants, animals, and nearby people."

Joelle and Ram look at each other to see who will share next. Neither one can decide, so they play a round of rock, paper, scissors, with Joelle having paper and Ram having a rock.

"I get to go next," Joelle cheers excitedly as Ram rolls his eyes playfully. "When I was eight, my parents took me to the Mediterranean Sea. They needed to go there for work. My mother was writing a paper about the history of all the different cultures surrounding the sea, and my father was buying things to sell in the U.S. I remember swimming in the blue water; it was so clear and warm. I got to snorkel and saw sea urchins, starfish, colored fish, and even dolphins. I also got to see the coral reefs, which are the home of so much marine life!" Joelle finished sharing with a huge smile as she motions her hand towards Ram, giving him the okay to start his story.

Ram begins talking about his experience with aquatic eco-systems. "My parents took me boating in the Pacific Ocean last summer. The ocean is so big and the water is deep; it seems like a bottomless ocean to me. We got to see whales spouting water into the air. We also saw dolphins jumping, and they even raced our boat; that was really fun! Our captain told us about the Pacific; he said that the ocean has tiny plankton you can barely see, turtles, and even sharks." Just as Ram finishes sharing, Ms. Olive rings her bell, letting the students know it is time to get ready for lunch.

Everyone finishes putting their books away while Ms. Olive shares another announcement with the class. "Everyone, I need your attention for a moment. I am assigning a research project for each table group. The project will be focused on ecosystems. However, I will allow the groups to decide what to research." Just then, the bell for lunch goes off, and students who brought their lunch from home grab their bags and everyone gets in line by the door, waiting for Ms. Olive's dismissal.

CHAPTER FIVE

Ecosystems Landfilled

It's lunchtime, and Jessica waits for the other students to leave the classroom. Once alone with Ms. Olive, she asks, "Ms. Olive, do you need any help today during lunch? I can help you."

Ms. Olive looks at Jessica with gentle eyes and a kind smile. "No, I have to run an errand, so I must leave the school campus during lunch. I think you should get some fresh air and hang out with the other students."

Ms. Olive guides Jessica to the door. "I will see you after lunch."

Jessica leaves the classroom feeling defeated. She has no choice but to eat outside with the other students. Jessica feels so embarrassed that she has no friends to sit with as she starts to walk toward an empty bench. As she begins to eat, she can hear the students gossiping about her.

"She's weird."

"She was found in the trash."

"She's dirt. Or trash girl. Gutter girl."

"She was meant to be homeless."

"Her real mom didn't want her."

"Well, look at her; she's so weird."

Jessica can hear them clearly since the students aren't trying to whisper—they don't care if she can hear them. Jessica loses her appetite and puts her food away, holding back her tears. She picks up her belongings from the bench and begins to walk away. She hears the voices of the other students in her mind.

Jessica walks with her head down away from the group of gossiping bullies. She is not looking where she is going and bumps into a garbage bin on the blacktop of the school yard. She suddenly jolts and sees images of landfills with what people call "trash." She sees the food breaking down and leaking gasses into the atmosphere. She sees objects that once belonged in the most beautiful places on the planet now covered in toxins in a huge hole in the earth. She sees a dark shadow and a black substance growing in the massive hole of what is called "trash."

She is completely captivated by her visions of what the students throw away as trash. She can see the original resources and what parts of the ecosystems they came from. She is unaware that her strange fixation on the garbage can has attracted an audience when a voice interrupts her daze.

Ram is the first to speak, breaking Jessica out of her daze. "Hi Jessica, what are you looking at?" Curious, Ram peeks over Jessica's shoulder to see what she is staring at. He sees nothing but the usual in the bin: cans, water bottles, paper, napkins, candy wrappers, food scraps, and other things. "What is so interesting in there? You see something I don't?"

Jessica slowly becomes aware of her surroundings and gets a little shy and embarrassed at the same time. She slowly turns around and shakes her head. She keeps her head down, embarrassed to look at the two students in front of her, afraid of their judgment. "That bin has valuable resources that have come from the most amazing places on this earth, and the process is hurting the life and the environment—habitats, delicate ecosystems, homes for the animal kingdom, our oceans, the mountains... The "trash" we throw away doesn't just go away; it doesn't disappear. The trash ends up in big holes in the ground. The trash doesn't get recycled or composted. Instead, it just sits there, breaking down and leaking gross stuff. The landfills are releasing gasses and toxins into the air, and that causes diseases in neighborhoods close to them. There's dark, oily sludge that's poison, and some of the older landfills leak it into the ground, the surrounding soil, and into the water. We're hurting the planet with the things we throw away; we're making the planet sick. It's awful; it's so awful."

Joelle is standing next to Ram, looking at Jessica, a little shocked by what Jessica is saying about the trash can. She waits for Jessica to finish and decides to share her thoughts on trash. "Yes, it is a problem. I have done a little bit of research on this issue about consumerism and waste. It's not good."

With panic in her voice, Jessica continues, "It's not just the **landfills**, but there are these huge machines that burn stuff too."

Ram quickly shares, "Oh, you mean **incinerators**. They have a lot of those in India."

Jessica nods. "Those machines burn the trash to get rid of it, but it leaves this toxic ash. The leftover ash has to go somewhere, so they bury it, putting more toxins into the earth. The smoke is toxic, too. Burning the trash creates toxic chemicals that are going into the air, poisoning the air we breathe." Jessica looks at Joelle and Ram with concern. "Every piece of trash was once a part of our beautiful planet: a tree, a mountain, the ocean, the ground, the home for other life. When we don't take care of our stuff, our stuff turns into something horrible and dangerous to us all. We have to do something about it; we have to stop it. We have to do something better than throwing everything away and get everyone to understand. It's so important."

Ram and Joelle look at each other for a moment. Without words, they both look at Jessica and then back at each other. Ram whispers in Joelle's ear, and she nods her head yes. Ram looks back at Jessica and asks, "Maybe we can do our research project on wasted resources from the different ecosystems?"

Jessica is still feeling overwhelmed, sad, and embarrassed. Trying to hold back her tears, she says quietly, "Oh ... okay."

Ram continues to talk to Jessica, trying to support her the best way he knows how. He says, "We've seen you around the last couple of days in school alone. Do you have any friends?"

Joelle is shocked by Ram's bluntness and is concerned that it hurts Jessica's feelings. Joelle sends Ram a sharp look. "Ram, seriously?!" She then tries to correct her friend's brutal honesty. "What he means is, we have seen you alone a lot and wonder if you have anyone to have lunch with."

Jessica looks at the ground and shakes her head slowly, saying no, trying to hold back the choking sensation that makes her want to cry.

Ram and Joelle look at Jessica, who is trying her hardest to hold back tears. Joelle gives Jessica a soft hug and looks over at Ram. "Well, you can hang with us," Joelle says with conviction. They both take Jessica by her arms, link theirs with hers, each of them on the opposite side of Jessica, and walk united toward class.

Joelle says cheerfully, "Let's go back to class."

CHAPTER SIX:
Wasted Resources

Jessica, Ram, and Joelle agree to do their intensive research together over the next couple of weekends about wasted resources and how they impact the balance within the planet's ecosystems. Each week, they rotate which house they meet to do research, discuss their findings, and organize how to present their discoveries to Ms. Olive and their classmates.

This particular Saturday, the three students decide to meet at Joelle's house. Joelle's home is the biggest on the block, located at the corner of the street. It is Victorian architecture, painted with soft cream, blue, forest green, and gold, and it looks like a castle.

Grandma Charlotte drops Jessica off at the tree-lined driveway just as Ram's mother pulls up behind her car. Both Jessica and Ram get out of their family cars, say goodbye to their family, and walk to greet each other.

Both Jessica and Ram walk together and approach the house's

front porch with hanging flower baskets. As they walk up the steps to the oak front door with golden knobs, Joelle opens the door, smiling at them. "Hi Jessica. Hi Ram. Welcome to my home."

Joelle guides her friends inside her home. Jessica's eyes light up when she sees the inside of Joelle's house, which has high ceilings, antique furniture, golden-framed artwork on the walls, and a giant staircase that makes the house seem like it came straight out of an old classic movie. The house smells of freshly baked cookies and fresh berry pies.

Joelle grins as she notices Jessica and Ram sniffing the yummy aroma in the air. "My mom baked us some treats that we can eat after lunch. My mom said lunch would be ready in an hour, but we can start our research now. Follow me; I will take you to my study room."

Joelle's study room is at the back of the house. It has big windows that look out into her backyard, which is filled with flowers, grass, a big oak tree, and a white statue of Chloris, the Greek goddess of spring and flowers.

Joelle, Ram, and Jessica all sit at a table in the center of the room and pull out books from the library to begin their research. Joelle pulls out her notepad and writes down some of her thoughts. "I think we need to research the basic material types that are easy to recycle that we see in the trash cans at school, like paper, plastic, metal, and sometimes glass jars. We need to explain what resources they come from and what happens to the ecosystems. Who wants to research paper?"

Jessica raises her hand, and Joelle nods her head in agreement.

She writes Jessica's name down on her notepad. Joelle looks up at Ram. "How about metal and glass?"

Ram nods, accepting his assignment. Joelle continues to talk. "Good, I will research plastic. Let's see how much information we can find before lunch."

All three of them begin to go through books and copies of articles and take notes.

An hour later, Joelle's mother's voice is heard from the kitchen. "Kids, lunch will be ready in fifteen minutes. You all should take a break soon."

Jessica, Ram, and Joelle all look up from their notes. Ram speaks first. "I have some notes that I am ready to share."

Jessica joins in. "Me too. I'm ready."

Joelle moves her pad of paper to the side, and she looks at Jessica and Ram. "Okay, let's share what we learned before lunch."

Ram shares his research: "75% of the world's metal production comes from Australia, Brazil, China, and India. Australia leads with the world's top mining, extracting metals like iron ore, aluminum, gold, copper, lithium, and more. Many metals are found in ores within the Earth's crust, mixed with minerals and rocks."

Joelle and Jessica both look at Ram, listening to the facts. Joelle adds, "This is a good start. How is the ore collected?

Does it harm ecosystems?"

Ram nods. "Yes, one of the most harmful practices used to mine is called **mountaintop removal**. The tops of mountains are literally removed by explosives to get to the metal ores, leaving a large, flat area. The mountaintop that is removed—the debris—is called '**overburden**,' which is dumped into nearby valleys."

Jessica speaks out softly. "Oh my. That sounds horrible."

Ram nods his head again. "It is horrible. Sometimes, the 'overburden' can bury streams and even pollute water from the heavy metals leaking into it, hurting the local ecosystems and increasing the possibility of flooding. All of this can contaminate the drinking water for the communities nearby."

Ram, Jessica, and Joelle are silent for a moment as they look at the glasses of water Joelle's mother left at the table for them to drink while they work.

Ram continues with a serious tone. "Mountaintop removal destroys forests, and the damage from the mining is permanent—the forest doesn't grow back after the removal."

"Oh no," Jessica and Joelle both say together in dismay.

"There's more—glass production can also harm the planet and people processing the raw materials," Ram says with concern. "Glass is made from **silica sand**, which is mined in places like North America, such as areas in Wisconsin, Iowa, and Illinois. Silica sand is also found in natural things like sand and stone.

It can be found in India, Japan, China, Indonesia, and Australia. It can also be found on white sand beaches like Siesta Key in Florida. There are a few industries where silica sand is used: glassmaking, metal casting, ceramics, water filtration, oil and gas drilling, and construction."

Joelle quickly adds, "Yes, I read that silica sand is used in hydraulic fracturing to extract oil and natural gas and can cause air and water *pollution*."

Ram nods. "Yes, and silica dust can be dangerous to human health. The dust is created from cutting, grinding, and crushing the crystalline silica, and it becomes 100 times smaller than sand. When the silica dust is inhaled, it can cause health problems like lung cancer and other respiratory diseases."

Joelle encourages Ram to continue by asking him, "Did you find out how silica sand is turned into glass?"

Ram continues looking at his notes. "Yes, I did. By heating the silica sand, also known as quartz sand, using temperatures above 3,090 degrees Fahrenheit, to be exact. This melts the sand into a clear liquid that can be cooled quickly, molding the silica quickly into the shape needed."

Joelle looks at Ram and says, "Good job. I think we will have a good report for Ms. Olive."

Ram notices Jessica looking down at the table to avoid eye contact, and he takes the hint that she is not ready to share yet. To give Jessica more time, he asks Joelle, "What did you find out about plastic?"

Joelle is eager to share her discoveries. "Plastic is created from raw materials, and the main ones are natural gas and crude oil, which are **fossil fuels**. Fossil fuels are crude oil, coal, and natural gas, and are nonrenewable resources."

Jessica looks up with curiosity and inquires softly, "What does nonrenewable mean?"

Joelle continues confidently, "**Nonrenewable** means that the natural resource cannot be replaced quickly enough to keep up with consumption and demand."

Jessica questions, "Why?"

Joelle answers, "You see, fossil fuels come from the remains of ancient animals and plants buried under layers of rock millions of years ago. Fossil fuels are used for many things all over the world, such as coal, which is used for electricity and transportation. Natural gas is used for heating, electricity, and for industrial use. Oil sand is used for roads, runways, planes, parking lots, and sidewalks. Crude oil is used for gasoline, fuel, chemicals, and plastic."

Jessica responds with shock, "Wow, we use fossil fuels for almost everything."

"Correct, the majority of the world depends on fossil fuel." Joelle continues to share what she researched, looking at her notes for more information. "The leading countries that extract oil are the United States, Saudi Arabia, Russia, and China. Fossil fuels are major contributors to climate change. When fossil fuels are burned, they release carbon dioxide and other **greenhouse**

gasses that trap heat from the sun in the Earth's atmosphere. What plastic is made from is **petroleum**, which comes from fossils of zooplankton and algae that have settled under layers of the bottom of oceans and lakes for millions of years."

Ram wants to know more. "Did you research how plastic is made?"

Joelle nods, "Yes, the process of making **plastic happens in five stages. The first stage is extraction**, where crude oil and natural gas are extracted from the ground or bottom of the ocean. The **second stage is transportation**, where these materials are taken to a refinery. The **third stage is the refining process**, where crude oil and natural gas are turned into ethane and propane. The **fourth process is called cracking**, where the ethane and propane are heated, breaking them down into ethylene and propylene. The **fifth stage is called polymerization**, where ethylene and propylene are combined with other chemicals to form polymers, which are the building blocks for different types of plastic. Polymers can be molded and shaped into plastic products."

Ram and Joelle look to Jessica to see if she is ready to share.

Jessica clears her throat, a little nervous to speak. "Trees are harvested for many reasons, including what we see thrown away at school daily: paper. Trees are used for building homes, creating furniture, creating tools, and for wood pulp to make paper."

Jessica pauses for a moment because she notices her hands are shaking.

Joelle can see that Jessica is nervous, and she does her best to encourage Jessica by sharing her own thoughts on the subject. "Yes, paper is used a lot at school. It is often used once and thrown away. I see so much paper in the trash cans at school. This is good; please keep sharing, Jessica."

Jessica nods her head and looks down at the paper with her notes. "Paper makes up 26% of landfill waste, with newspapers alone making up 13%. 42% of the wood harvested is used to make paper. The process of making paper uses a lot of energy, water, and fossil fuels like oil. The paper industry is the third largest consumer of fossil fuels in the world."

Ram says, surprised, "Wow, I didn't know that making paper would use so much oil."

Jessica continues with concern in her voice. "Yes, and there is more. Forests are cleared for agriculture to grow food. Farming has been one of the reasons for **deforestation** when trees are cut down faster than they can grow back."

Joelle is shocked. "What? Food production causes deforestation?!"

Jessica nods. "Yes, it does. Countries affected by deforestation are Nigeria, Honduras, the Philippines, and Indonesia. In fact, 90% of Nigeria's trees have been cut down."

Joelle asks another question. "Do you have more information on the forests that have been damaged by deforestation?"

Jessica continues reading from her notes and begins to share. "The largest rainforest in the world is the Amazon in Brazil, which stretches across 6.9 million square kilometers. The Amazon is the home of three million species of plants and animals and a million indigenous people. The forest covers 40% of South America, half of the Earth's remaining tropical forests. More than 40% of the global tropical deforestation happens in Brazil, where most of the Amazon is located. 1.5 million hectares of rainforest are lost annually, contributing to the 5 million hectares of forest destroyed globally. The leading causes of deforestation are agriculture, livestock farming, logging, and mining."

Ram grabs his calculator. "1.5 million hectares is equivalent to 3.7 million football fields of rainforest lost a year. This is in addition to the 12.35 million football fields of forests destroyed around the world!"

Just then, Joelle's mother calls out, "Kids, lunch is ready!"

Joelle, Ram, and Jessica all look toward the kitchen in silence.

Jessica continues with deep concern, "I think some of the food-production practices and food waste are hurting our planet."

Biodiversity
Types of Biodiversity
Genetic Biodiversity
Species Biodiversity
Ecosystem Biodiversity

CHAPTER SEVEN

The Other Side of the Trash Bin

Jessica, Ram, and Joelle are becoming extremely motivated by their research and continue to uncover what's happening to the planet. They research the extraction process of natural resources, leading to the destruction of delicate ecosystems and habitats and to the **resources' end-of-life cycle** when people throw materials away.

Monday finally arrives, and they are expected to present their research project to the class. Joelle and Ram are excited to share, and both are almost jumping in their seats to be picked to present first. Jessica, however, is extremely nervous to present because of her fear of making a mistake, and her hands are shaking and sweaty. Adding to Jessica's anxiety, Ms. Olive notices Joelle's and Ram's enthusiasm to present, so she selects their group to go first.

All three students stand up and walk to the front of their class with a cardboard presentation board that they decorated, full of visuals to support their report. They are allowed to hold note cards, plus they had practiced presenting in front of each other's family members multiple times. They are prepared to share what they learned about the four main resources that are used at school and at home: paper, metal, glass, and plastic. They speak for about five minutes, explaining where the materials come from and how they are extracted and processed.

Jessica's heart beats loudly as she hears Joelle's voice and waits for her turn to speak. Joelle continues to explain, pointing to the landfill bin in the classroom. "Most people don't think about where all the resources go after they throw them away. Our trash ends up in the landfill. Landfills are not a smart solution for waste because they harm people and the environment. They are toxic."

The three of them take turns speaking, splitting the presentation among each other. It is Ram's turn to speak next. "Over 181 million tons of metal were mined worldwide in 2021, and 40% was aluminum. Metal is recyclable, but it still ends up in landfills. 10.53 million tons of steel and 2.66 million tons of aluminum make up about 8.76% of the total waste thrown into landfills. When metal is wasted, it's wasting mountains, ecosystems, habitats, and natural resources."

Ram points to a comparison picture of a mountain surrounded by a flourishing habitat next to a picture where the landscape has been stripped away, leaving a flattened, dramatically disrupted ecosystem. His finger then points to the next picture: a white-sand beach. "The world makes around 130 million tons of glass yearly, and container glass makes up 48% of that total. Glass is 100% recyclable, and yet it is still thrown away into the landfill. In the United States, 7.6 million tons of glass end up in the landfill. Only 32% of container glass and 11% of flat glass get recycled worldwide. Glass in the landfill is another example of wasted habitats and resources."

Joelle steps forward and points to a picture of an industrial structure surrounded by cranes towering over waves: an oil rig in the ocean. "The world produces over 430 million tons of plastic yearly. Half of the plastic ends up in landfills. What a waste of ancient fossil fuels, which are nonrenewable."

Jessica is next once again. She clears her throat, gripping her note cards for dear life. "Paper is also used all around the world, and 409 million metric tons of paper were made globally in 2018. In the United States, only 38% gets recycled, and 56% of cardboard and paper ends up in landfills. What a waste of our trees and our forests." Jessica pauses for a moment and takes a few steps closer to the presentation board, pointing to a picture of a vast landscape stripped of trees—a clear-cut forest that looks like a scarred earth expanding out from where a dense forest was once present. "Food production also puts pressure on our planet and ecosystems. Food is a process, and most people don't think about where their fruits and vegetables are grown or how the animals are raised for meat, milk, and eggs. Most people don't think about how the food gets processed and transported to stores and restaurants."

Ram takes over for a moment as they had planned. "Our food needs resources like sunlight, water, and land. Agriculture is one of the causes of deforestation. Trees are friends of the planet. They absorb carbon dioxide and produce the oxygen we breathe through photosynthesis. When trees are cut down, they release carbon into the atmosphere, increasing global warming."

Jessica lifts a cardboard circle graph displaying the facts she shares. "In the United States, we use 80% of our drinking water and 50% of our livable land for farming. That means land and water are no longer available for wildlife. Deforestation destroys animal habitats, reduces biodiversity, and leads to problems like soil erosion and water pollution."

Joelle holds up an apple. "The world's global food system is the main driver for biodiversity loss. **Biodiversity loss** means a decline of the variety of all living things on our planet, leading to the extinction of a population or a species globally. Of the 28,000 species, 24,000, which is 86%, are at risk of extinction due to agriculture alone."

Jessica holds up another cardboard picture with more graphs and examples. "There is a lot of sacrifice that goes into food production so people on the planet have food, and yet 30-40% of food is wasted. To better understand how much food is wasted, imagine we brought a large pizza to school and threw away 3 or 4 good slices into the trash. That's how much edible food is wasted every day. When edible food is thrown away, it's also throwing away the water, the land, and the energy that went into making the food, and dismissing the fact that food productions can cause biodiversity loss and destruction of natural habitats."

Joelle walks over to the classroom trash can and pretends to throw away her apple. "If food waste were a country, it would be the third largest emission contributor in the world. Landfills release methane gas, a very harmful greenhouse gas.

When organic waste, like food, plants, and paper, decomposes without oxygen, it creates methane gas."

Ram joins in after Joelle's theatrical demonstration, pointing back to the presentation board to a picture of the planet's atmosphere. "**Methane** gas is 84 times more effective at trapping heat than carbon dioxide emitted from cars, and methane can stay in the atmosphere up to 100 years or longer." Ram then directs the class to look at a picture of a landfill. "Landfills need space, and we have to clear natural habitats to build landfills. The average size of a landfill is 600 acres."

Jessica joins in, finally feeling a little more confident about speaking since they are getting close to the end of the presentation. "In the United States, there are over 3,000 landfills in operation and 10,000 closed. 3,000 landfills mean 1.8 million acres of habitats lost. Wildlife is kicked out of its homes and the ecosystems are destroyed."

Ram points to a picture of massive amounts of trash stretching over a large area of land with birds flying above, the piles of waste containing a mixture of materials, including food waste, plastic, metal, paper, and other debris. "**Landfills** are big holes in the ground where everything that gets buried will never be recycled or composted. They have plastic or clay liners that are meant to prevent toxic waste from leaking into the ground."

Joelle chimes in with a dramatic voice, pointing to a diagram that shows the landfill in the ground and all the operational and functional components of the structure. "But the liners can still leak over time, releasing a toxic liquid called leachate that can contaminate drinking water, nearby streams, lakes, and ponds.

Leachate contains chemicals like ammonia and mercury."

Jessica continues, "When ammonia gets into water sources, it can cause **eutrophication**, a process where nutrients accumulate in the water, resulting in an increased growth of plants that removes the oxygen in the water. Eutrophication creates **dead zones** where there's a lack of oxygen and animals can't survive. Landfills are a problem for human health, too. There have been studies that show children born near hazardous-waste landfills have a 12% increased risk of birth defects."

Joelle jumps in front of Ram and Jessica and is excited to share. "Our solution is to talk to the principal and start a green team. We want to set up green bins in the lunchroom to separate food waste and food solid paper, like paper plates, paper cups, and paper napkins and towels, so the resources can be composted instead of turned into methane."

Ram continues with the final announcement. "We want to set up blue recycling bins in the lunchroom, on campus, and in the classroom. We want to help capture all that can be recycled, save resources from entering landfills and harming our planet, and reduce the demands for resources to be extracted from vulnerable habitats."

Jessica finishes the presentation with a sound of relief in her voice. "We want to lead a call to action around campus for everyone to reduce their waste. We can help the planet by using reusables as much as possible, like bringing our own water bottles to school or packing our lunches in reusable containers."

Ms. Olive is quite impressed and the first person in the

classroom to clap her hands. "Wow, that was quite informative, you three. You even went above and beyond with your research with a call to action. I am quite impressed and would love to support your school initiative in any way I can."

Joelle, Ram, and Jessica look at each other and smile because they have already discussed asking Ms. Olive for her help.

Jessica speaks up, shy to ask in front of her class but eager to ask Ms. Olive the big question. "Ms. Olive, Joelle, Ram, and I were hoping you would be our green team teacher. We researched what we need to have an official club at school, and it includes a teacher's support. Will you help us?"

Ms. Olive smiles hugely and humbly responds, "It would be an honor to help you all. We can discuss the next steps during lunch."

Jessica, Ram, and Joelle are so excited that they all jump into the air and give each other a high five. At that moment, Jessica forgets why she was so nervous and confidently returns to her seat.

The rest of the class goes by fast. Three other groups present, and then it's time for recess. Instead of being alone this time, Jessica goes outside to socialize with her two new best friends, Joelle and Ram.

Compost
Recycling
Garbage

CHAPTER EIGHT

Green Team
Citizen Scientists

Jessica, Joelle, Ram, and Ms. Olive start working on creating their school's green team and have a meeting during lunch.

Ms. Olive sits at her desk taking notes while Jessica, Ram, and Joelle sit at desks directly in front of hers. The students have their notes to help prepare for their pitch to the principal and custodian. Ms. Olive asks her first question. "What should our club mission be?"

Jessica, Joelle, and Ram look at each other, smiling because they had prepared for this meeting and these questions while working on the finishing touches of their presentation. Jessica clears her throat and reads from her notes: "We feel our mission should be to help our school become environmentally sustainable by helping reduce the school's overall waste."

Ms. Olive nods. "Very good." She writes these notes and asks, "How do we plan to accomplish this?"

Joelle raises her hand to answer. "We need to set up the 'infrastructure'—that's what my dad says." Joelle blushes and continues to share. "Currently, there is no recycling or compost service, and everything is going to the landfill. We did some research and discovered that if we change what is being thrown away into the school's trash dumpster to the right bins, like recycling and compost, the school will save money. We found a local company with cheaper garbage service prices for recycling and composting." Joelle gets up and brings a printed paper to Ms. Olive's desk.

Ram pulls out another printed sheet of paper with pictures of blue, green, and gray recycling bins of various sizes. He walks over and puts the paper on Ms. Olive's desk. "We would like to suggest installing the proper bins on campus for recycling in the classrooms, composting food waste in the lunchroom, and collecting recyclables. This will help us reduce garbage at school."

Ms. Olive looks at the papers brought to her desk. She reads them and begins to think. There is silence for a couple of minutes as Ms. Olive flips through the pages and writes down notes. Joelle, Ram, and Jessica wait patiently, looking at Ms. Olive as she reviews their school waste recycling proposal. Finally, Ms. Olive says, "Some of the changes you are requesting will need to be approved by Mr. Greene, the custodian, and Principal Rodgers."

Jessica smiles and says, "Sure, we can ask Mr. Greene. I help him clean up after lunch when people leave stuff around the cafeteria. He likes me!"

Ms. Olive frowns momentarily at the information she hears. "If students aren't picking up after themselves, it may be harder to convince them to sort their waste."

There's another moment of silence, and the bell rings, signaling lunch is over.

Ms. Olive speaks up in order to finish their first green team meeting with a to-do list for the students. "We will need to get Mr. Greene's approval to make changes in the school's waste, because it's his job to empty all the trash cans. We may be adding more work for him, and that is not fair. We will also need to get the okay from Principal Rodgers. He will only say yes if we can promise that the school will follow along with the changes, so you all will have to come up with a plan to get the school and students to agree to participate with the green team's plans for the school."

Ram, Joelle, and Jessica look at each other and nod their heads as they accept their first green team challenge.

The following week, Jessica, Joelle, and Ram convince Mr. Greene to allow them to do their first waste audits. The purpose of a waste audit is to gather all the information on what is being thrown away into the landfill during lunchtime and around campus. Mr. Greene saves sample bags from the cafeteria and from a few different classrooms. He gives the students a tarp, extra bins to sort the materials, and gloves to keep their hands from directly touching the wasted materials.

Joelle, Jessica, and Ram all meet after school to begin the waste audit. Ms. Olive has a hand scale, clipboard with a pen, paper, and camera to take before and after pictures of the waste after it has been sorted.

The students start with the hardest stuff to sort first: the trash bags from the lunch rooms. The three bags from the lunch room are surprisingly heavy; bag number 1 weighs 10 pounds, bag number 2 weighs 6 pounds, and bag number 3 weighs 8 pounds. The students decide to break down the bags one at a time. They pull a lot of food waste and place it into a bin with a plastic liner bag, then do the same for all the recycling, putting it into another bin, then place the actual trash into a third bin. They weigh each bag's contents and sort them into three categories: compost, recycle, and landfill. The average result is that most of the weight comes from food waste, second is recycling, and the landfill bag is the lightest. They discover that their school's food waste is about 50% of the entire weight from the bags, while recycling is 30%, and landfill is 5%. Something that the students did not expect to find was uneaten food and food still sealed in packaging, which makes up 15% of the waste in weight.

Jessica remarks about the unopened and uneaten food: "It doesn't make sense why people throw away good food." She picks up an unopened chocolate oat bar. "They could have saved this for later, and if they don't like eating it, they should tell their parents."

Ms. Olive agrees. "Yes, some of these students are throwing away their parents' money by not eating the food or communicating that they don't want it."

Joelle chimes in, "This should be a part of our green team

campaign to raise awareness and focus on why this habit should change. The ecosystems have been damaged to make the food available for us to eat, and then just to throw it away is so sad."

Ram moves the research along. "Let's look and see what is being thrown away in the classroom."

They spend a few more minutes sorting a couple of bags from a few different classrooms and see immediate patterns. The bags contain mostly paper towels, writing paper from the classrooms, and a few glue sticks, pens, and pencils.

Ram looks at the sorted waste from the classrooms. "It looks like it's mostly paper being thrown away."

Jessica adds, "Yes, but the paper towels can't be recycled because paper can only be recycled seven times. Paper towels, tissues, and napkins are the last recycling cycle."

Joelle concludes, "Well, we need to compost the paper towels then. We don't want them in the landfill; they will just turn into methane."

Everyone nods in agreement. Jessica's eyes light up as a thought pops into her head. "If that is the case, then we need to compost the paper towels in the bathroom, too!"

Ms. Olive directs Joelle and Jessica to look into a few girls' bathrooms and peek into the trash cans to confirm what is being thrown away. She asked Ram to do the same for the boys' bathrooms. She then heads off to the staff bathrooms to inspect the trash bins in the school office building.

All four meet back in Ms. Olive's room to discuss the final results from the school waste audit. Jessica, Ram, and Joelle sit back at their desks facing Ms. Olive.

Ms. Olive asks the first question: "What do you think is the number one category of waste thrown away at school?"

The room is silent for a moment, and then Jessica raises her hand. "Well, the lunch room waste audit had more compostable waste than recycling and landfill waste. There was a lot of compostable paper that had food on it. When Joelle and I went to look at the three girls' bathrooms, we saw mostly paper towels in the trash can, and they were full. I think compost is the number one category of waste."

Ms. Olive is taking down notes. "What do you all think is the second category of waste?"

Ram raises his hand to speak. "I would say recycling is second. We saw a lot of paper in the classrooms and the lunchroom: milk cartons, juice boxes, some aluminum and plastic containers, and cardboard prepackaged lunch boxes. I also looked over the dumpster outside, and I saw a lot of cardboard boxes. Those are recyclable, too."

Ms. Olive continues to write notes. "Our next step is to present all the facts to Mr. Greene and see what he says."

Save The Blue Macaw

CHAPTER NINE

Green Teams
Save the Blue Macaw

Joelle, Ram, and Jessica meet once again over the weekend to discuss their waste audit results and do more research. They want to make sure the report they share with Mr. Greene is full of convincing information and facts. If Mr. Greene agrees to sign off on the plan to compost and recycle at school, then the green team can take the plan to Principal Rodgers.

Monday finally arrives, and Jessica, Ram, and Joelle meet Mr. Greene and Ms. Olive before school starts. They are prepared to share their report.

Joelle starts sharing the facts. "When we did the waste audit from the bags in the lunchroom, bathroom, and some of the classrooms, we uncovered many surprising details. 50% of the school's waste is compostable, including food scraps, solid paper, and paper towels. That is a lot of waste headed to the landfill, which turns into methane that hurts our planet. We want to fix this and help our school be a part of the solution."

Joelle looks to Ram for him to start his share. Ram holds his notes and says, "Recycling is the second on the list of materials we can save from entering the landfill. 30% of the waste at school is paper, but we think that is split between 15% paper towels, which are compost, and 20% recyclable paper, like reading and writing paper, the cardboard boxes I saw in the dumpster, and the lunchroom milk cartons, juice boxes, and cardboard prepackaged lunch boxes. About 10% of the recyclables are plastic trays from the prepackaged lunch boxes, yogurt, pudding, and applesauce cups. There was also a little bit of metal, like aluminum."

Ram looks to Jessica because it's her turn to speak. Jessica is confidently holding her notes, and all the public speaking lately has started to boost her self-esteem. "Not recycling milk cartons and juice boxes hurts our planet. Milk cartons are 88% paper and juice boxes are 74% paper. We calculated that the school dumps 391 full trash bags of cartons a year. That's like throwing away trees that were once wildlife habitats and wasting the biodiversity that was lost in order to create these materials."

Mr. Greene agrees. "Yes, what you share sounds accurate with what I see being thrown away every day at school."

Jessica smiles confidently and says, "Mr. Greene, we have decided to make the blue macaw our green team mascot."

Joelle adds, "The blue macaw is a native bird in the Amazon rainforest, and its species is becoming endangered due to illegal logging, agricultural land clearing, and land development. Not composting or recycling is participating in destroying our natural habitats, and we want our school to take a stand and become environmentally responsible."

Mr. Greene, in agreement, also shares his concerns. "I understand what you are saying. But the students here barely clean up after themselves; they litter. Not only that, but all the extra recycle bins will make more work for me. I don't have the extra time."

Ram shares the green team plan. "Do not worry, Mr. Greene. We plan to help you. We plan to have big blue cans in all the quads at school. The green team will be responsible for emptying the recycle bins from the classrooms into the bin in the quad, helping reduce the work."

Mr. Greene questions, "What about getting the students to sort?"

Joelle shares, "We want to get Principal Rodgers's support. We will work on our Save the Blue Macaw campaign. We propose to share with the entire school how litter hurts our planet. We hope more classmates will join our green team to help."

Mr. Greene looks at the three students and then at Ms. Olive and says, "Well, you all seem very passionate about this. I agree with you all that the waste at this school is not good. I will agree to help—under one condition, though: as long as you get the school to participate and help with the recycling around the school campus."

"We promise!" Joelle, Ram, and Jessica say in unison. They shake Mr. Greene's hand.

Ms. Olive smiles and looks at Mr. Greene. "Thank you for your support. I will also try to get other teachers on board and Principal Rodgers's support."

The following week, Ms. Olive, Mr. Greene, Jessica, Joelle, and Ram brainstorm a plan of action to share with Principal Rodgers. They combine the student report on the wasted resources and habitats impacted by natural resource extraction. They also include the school waste audit results from the week before.

Mr. Rodgers sits at his desk, listening quietly to all the details the students share with him. The team also gives him a paper with the same facts to help him keep up since they have a lot of information.

"Our school has 500 students, and by recycling, we would save around 780,000 sheets of paper," Jessica's voice filled Mr. Rodgers' office. "That's around 72 trees and around 29,800 gallons of water, and avoiding 1,956 trash bags sent to the landfill a year."

Mr. Greene shares all his calculations. "With 50% of the waste being composted and 30% being recycled, there will be fewer trash pickups and lower waste management costs. The trash dumpster size can be reduced, and the compost and recycling are cheaper. We will actually save the school money."

Ms. Olive adds, "By allowing the school to recycle and compost, our school will be environmentally responsible and give the students the right message that it's important to respect the planet and conserve resources."

Principal Rodgers looks at the group standing in front of his desk. He stands up, looks everyone in the eyes, and smiles. "Thank you for sharing this information with me. I agree with you all that it is important that we do something about reducing our waste at school and practice being more sustainable. If we succeed, I will agree to make our school a district pilot. I will help you all present to the school board, and maybe we can support the school district in making similar changes."

The office is filled with instant cheers from the group as they take their first step toward creating positive change.

That night, Jessica sits on her bed, ready to sleep. She is happy with everything that is happening at school. She now has two friends she adores, and she is working with Ms. Olive, Mr. Greene, and Principal Rodgers to help her school become more sustainable. However, a bit of sadness also lingers as she looks outside her window to Grandma's Secret Garden. She hasn't spoken to her nature friends in weeks. As she touches the window, she softly says, "Maybe one day soon, I can introduce you to my new friends."

CHAPTER TEN:
Wasted Resources
Water and Land, Part I

Mr. Greene and the official green team get to work immediately and walk around the school to decide how many bins to order and where to place them around campus. Joelle, Ram, and Jessica team up with Ms. Olive to create signs with pictures of the example materials that go in each bin for the school. The green team meets with Principal Rodgers to schedule an assembly the week after all the bins are expected to arrive on campus. The assembly allows the green team to introduce their school recycling program and explain why school sorting is important. Both Principal Rodgers and Mr. Greene agree that littering is a problem at school, so they ask the green team to add it to their assembly, explaining why litter hurts the planet.

Ms. Olive supports Joelle, Ram, and Jessica with the litter assignment by scheduling the green team to participate in a weekend litter pickup and visit to the Monterey Bay Aquarium.

Finally, Saturday arrives—a big day for Jessica, so she gets up early this morning. Joelle, Ram, and her are meeting with

Ms. Olive for a bay litter pickup and a trip to the Monterey Bay Aquarium. She pulls out layers of clothes to wear to prepare for a cold morning that can transform into a warmer day, just as Ms. Olive suggested. There is an aroma of pancakes coming from the kitchen, so she hurries, gets dressed, and joins her grandmother in the kitchen.

"Good morning, Jessica. Breakfast is ready. Are you excited about your trip today?" Grandma Charlotte looks at her granddaughter with love in her eyes as she hands Jessica a plate of warm pancakes.

Jessica takes the plate and walks to the dining room to eat, and Grandma Charlotte follows with her own plate of pancakes. Jessica sits down and grabs the maple syrup on the table. "Yes, I am. This is an important trip. Joelle, Ram and I need to collect information to share with the school about why littering hurts our planet. We need to connect this information with our request for the school to recycle and compost."

"Oh, I see," Grandma Charlotte says with amusement.

Jessica continues to share her opinion. "We already know that throwing away materials that could be composted or recycled into the landfill harms the planet, that the waste in landfills is made of resources that came from natural habitats, and this harms many ecosystems. Now, we need to research what happens to natural habitats when materials are littered."

Grandma Charlotte listens to Jessica speak while she quietly chews her food. After a moment, she responds, "Well, I look forward to hearing about what type of litter you discover and what you uncover about the impacts litter has on our local environment."

Jessica quickly finishes her food so she can get ready to leave. She brings her dishes to the sink and begins to wash them. Grace enters the kitchen just as Jessica puts her plate and utensils in the drying rack.

Grace greets her mother and Jessica as she enters the kitchen. "Good morning; Breakfast smells good." Grace walks up to Jessica as she finishes cleaning up and hugs her. Just as she turns to give her mother a hug, Charlotte hands her a plate of pancakes.

Grace holds the plate in one hand and hugs her mother with her free arm. "Thank you! The pancakes look delicious."

"They are," Jessica says as she starts to make her way out of the kitchen.

Grace responds quickly to Jessica's exit from the kitchen. "What's happening today? Why are you in a rush?"

"Ms. Olive agreed to pick Ram, Joelle, and me up to carpool to our first green team citizen scientist investigation on litter. She should be here any minute now," Jessica says from down the hall.

"Oh, that's right. I forgot." Grace takes her plate into the dining room to eat. Charlotte brings Grace a cup of coffee, sits down at the table with her daughter, and slowly begins sipping coffee from her cup.

Jessica comes back into the dining room. This time, she has everything she needs for the day: her reusable water bottle, backpack, and jacket. She walks up to Grace and Charlotte at the table and gives each a kiss on the cheek and a hug goodbye. "Ms. Olive is outside. I will be back later."

"I look forward to hearing about your adventure when you get back," Grandma Charlotte says, smiling at Jessica as she leaves out the door.

Charlotte and Grace can see the front yard of their house and Ms. Olive's car outside. Both Ram and Joelle are standing outside next to the back door of the car. They greet Jessica, each giving her a hug, and all three get into the backseat, close the car door, and drive away.

Grace takes a bite of her pancake and looks at the car driving down the street until it's out of sight. "It's such a relief that she finally made real friends. I was beginning to worry about her."

Charlotte speaks up in defense of her granddaughter. "I always knew she would make friends eventually. I never doubted her ability. To be honest, I found it quite innocent that Jessica had make-believe friends; she was using her imagination. I don't see what the rush was or is to have her grow up so quickly."

Grace takes a sip of her coffee and responds, "Mother, that is where we disagree."

Grace and Charlotte both look out the window and continue to drink their coffee in silence.

Ms. Olive takes the green team to meet with a group running a litter pickup by Martin Luther King Jr. Regional Shoreline, which is unfortunately known for extreme litter that leads directly into the Bay.

The group is greeted by a team of volunteers wearing yellow vests. The volunteers hand Joelle, Ram, Ms. Olive, and Jessica gloves, trash pickers, and buckets to pick up litter with. They are given instructions not to pick up anything sharp and to mark anything that can be potentially dangerous with flags they are given.

Ms. Olive leads Jessica, Ram, and Joelle toward a pathway that leads closer to the shoreline. They are all shocked by what they see: the extreme contrast between a beautiful habitat and the layers of litter that entwine and surround it. The shoreline has a mixture of seaweed and driftwood mingled with food wrappers, plastic bags, and plastic packaging. They notice the wildlife that has adapted to the litter. They see a bird nesting near a pile of trash.

Jessica points to another bird, a heron, nearby, picking through the trash and looking for food. "That's horrible; what if the bird eats some of the plastic?"

A woman volunteer wearing a yellow vest overhears Jessica's distressing words. "Unfortunately, many marine animals are injured or killed by plastic debris."

Jessica questions, "Plastic debris?"

The woman continues, "Yes, **plastic debris** is plastic that is found in natural environments without serving a purpose. For example, seaweed and a jellyfish have a purpose in the water, but a plastic bag does not."

Joelle joins the conversation. "Oh, plastic debris is another way to say litter?"

The woman looks at Joelle and smiles. "Yes, plastic debris is plastic materials out of place. A study has found that over 700 marine species have been confirmed to eat plastic. Another study reported that 267 species have been fatally impacted by plastic pollution worldwide. Both studies include fish, seabirds, turtles, and marine mammals."

Jessica starts walking toward a plastic water bottle littered on the edge of the trail. She picks up the bottle, and at that moment, Jessica looks over at the bird picking through plastic, and everything around her goes silent. Jessica gets overwhelmed by a cold sensation that washes over her body, and she is overcome by visions flashing before her eyes. She sees images in her mind of marine life suffering, being entangled in plastics, starving to death from eating plastics, animals extremely sick that are suffering from plastic poisoning, and animals drowning from being caught in plastic waste.

"Jessica, are you alright?" Ms. Olive's voice brings Jessica back to the present moment. Ms. Olive looks concerned as she notices Jessica's face has gone pale and tears are streaming from her eyes.

"Yes, Ms. Olive. I'm fine," Jessica says with a shaky voice. She takes a deep breath, trying to stop herself from crying about the visions she had just seen, and asks the woman to clarify what she means. "Do you mean they are dying?"

The woman continues, "Yes, plastic pollution is responsible for deaths among many kinds of marine life, including 86% of sea turtle species, 44% of seabird species, and 43% of marine mammal species."

Everyone goes silent and looks at the bird that is looking for food. The woman continues to share, motioning to the bird. "Seabirds that feed on the surface of the ocean suffer from ingesting plastic that floats. They mistake the plastics for food. The adult birds will feed the plastics to their baby chicks, and it's lowering their growth and survival rate."

"What about turtles?" Ram asks with concern. "Turtles are one of my favorite animals."

The woman's eyes get bigger, and she looks off into the Bay. "All seven species of turtles have been confirmed to eat plastic film and plastic bags. Unfortunately, the turtles can't tell the difference between plastic bags and jellyfish."

The woman notices Jessica wiping a tear that streamed down her cheek, and with compassion, she does her best to redirect the conversation. "Please, pardon my manners. I am Joan. I am one of the litter cleanup leads. Thank you all for joining us today."

Ms. Olive steps up to Joan, and they shake each other's gloved hands. "I'm Ms. Olive. These are my students: Ram, Joelle, and Jessica. They are my green team students, and we are putting together a sustainable school proposal to reduce our school's waste."

Joan smiles at Ram, Joelle, and Jessica. She looks back at Ms. Olive. "Thank you for your work and advocacy."

Ram sees a plastic bag stuck on a bush near the walking trail and runs over to it. He uses his trash picker to grab the bag and put the plastic waste into his bucket. Ram shouts over his shoulder to the group, "It's a good thing we are here to help!"

Joelle and Jessica follow Ram's lead and start picking up litter near the marsh. They see some food containers, plastic straws, styrofoam packaging, soda cans, and glass bottles stashed away in the shrubs. They also see a lot of broken-down plastic pieces.

In dismay, Joelle complains, "There are so many small plastics."

The woman volunteer is nearby and walks over to the girls, looking into Joelle's bucket. "Aha, microplastics. Yes, they are a huge problem."

Jessica questions, "Microplastics?"

Once again, Joan shares her knowledge of plastics with the girls. "**Microplastics** are those small, broken-down pieces of plastics you both are finding along the shoreline."

Jessica asks another question. "How are microplastics created?"

Joan explains, "Microplastics come from larger plastics that break apart into smaller pieces over time due to being in the elements like sunlight, water, waves, wind, and also from other things. They are a big problem for wildlife, our watershed, and our waterways. That's why these litter pickups are so important."

The girls nod their heads and continue to pick up as much as they can find. They spend an hour picking up litter. Ms. Olive, Ram, Joelle, and Jessica collect a lot of food packaging, like fast-food containers, plastic water bottles, soda cans, and chip bags.

Jessica picks up pieces of styrofoam that look like they have been there for a long time. She tries to examine one, and the styrofoam crumbles in her gloved hands. "This is crumbling into microplastics."

Ram is nearby, picking up a plastic bag tangled in marsh plants. He carefully pulls it out, saying, "I don't want any more animals to eat this stuff."

Ms. Olive, who is near the students but closer to the trail, says, "I can't believe how many cigarette butts I have been finding. They contain harmful chemicals that can leach into the water too." Ms. Olive looks at her watch and motions to the children. "It's time to start heading back to the group. The litter pickup is just about over, and we have a long drive to the Monterey Bay Aquarium."

They return to where all the volunteers are and bring back the litter pickup supplies. Joelle sees a broken plastic fork and picks it up. "I wonder how long it takes plastic to break down and return back to nature?"

One of the litter pickup leads responds to Joelle's question. "Plastic can take 500–1,000 years to break down, and it becomes microplastics, not fully degrading."

Ram, Joelle, and Jessica hand over their trash pickers and buckets of litter to the lead volunteers. They throw away their plastic gloves in the trash can nearby and, with nothing left to say, they follow Ms. Olive to the car.

CHAPTER ELEVEN:
Wasted Resources Water and Land, Part II

Ms. Olive drives along the scenic route, Highway 1, to the Monterey Bay Aquarium, so Jessica, Ram, and Joelle can observe the massive coastline that runs along the Pacific Ocean.

Once they arrive at the Monterey Bay Aquarium, they are welcomed by their tour guide, Angel. Angel has bleached blonde hair and a deep tan. "Hi everyone. My name is Angel, and I am your tour guide today. The health of the ocean is important to me. I am a professional surfer, and I enjoy surfing in clean water and seeing healthy marine life during my boating, snorkeling, and diving trips. Unfortunately, I have seen an increase in plastic in the Pacific Ocean in the last few decades. I decided to make a difference by educating people about our oceans, marine life, and delicate ecosystems. I hope you all will take this information back to share with your communities and lead the sustainable changes we need to see within our local and global communities."

Angel leads Ms. Olive, Ram, Jessica, and Joelle to the first exhibit, the kelp forest. The students stand in front of a massive tank that reaches all the way to the ceiling of the room. They stand there in awe, observing the kelp sway in the currents. They see a school of Pacific sardines swim by. Ram spots a bat ray and a leopard shark and points to them in amazement.

Angel's voice carries throughout the exhibit space. "The **kelp forest** is an essential habitat for many species of marine life in the Pacific. It's an underwater rainforest that produces oxygen and captures carbon dioxide. Plastic bags that drift in the ocean get tangled in the kelp, suffocating parts of the forest. Plastic pollution affects **phytoplankton photosynthesis** and growth as well as the zooplankton's development and reproduction."

Angel points to a display in the center of the space. "**Phytoplankton** are said to produce around 50% of the planet's oxygen. They use chlorophyll to absorb sunlight to convert carbon dioxide and water into oxygen. Phytoplankton are the 'plants of the ocean'—they capture carbon dioxide from the atmosphere and produce oxygen through the same photosynthetic process as land plants. The phytoplankton absorb carbon dioxide from the atmosphere through photosynthesis, storing it in the ocean."

Jessica raises her hand and Angel motions for her to speak. "Would phytoplankton be the producers in the marine ecosystem?"

Angel gets excited with the student engagement and replies, "Yes, they are. The **zooplankton** are the first consumers in the aquatic food chain; they eat the phytoplankton. Microplastics have a toxic effect on phytoplankton and zooplankton, which are the most important producers and consumers of the ocean."

Angel points to another graph that has the title "**Microplastic Biomagnification**." "This is the process of how microplastics move up the food chain and become more concentrated as they are consumed by predators." He points to the bottom of the graph with a picture of zooplankton. "When the zooplankton ingest microplastics and are eaten by larger fish, the plastic toxins accumulate in the fish bodies and get stored in the fat." He points to the next level above, which has a picture of bigger fish and marine animals labeled as predators. "The biomagnification process happens when the predator consumes prey. They ingest the plastics that have accumulated in the prey. As we move up the food chain, the concentration of the plastics and toxins increases."

Angel takes the group through other parts of the aquarium. Ram, Jessica, and Joelle enjoy watching sea otters playfully dive and float on their backs. The group sees the sea turtle exhibit, which compares plastic bags and jellyfish, demonstrating how turtles cannot see the difference.

The group moves into another hall with a huge picture that expands across one of the walls. It is a picture of the ocean that is polluted with plastic. The photograph's title is "The Great Pacific Garbage Patch," and in parentheses, "the Pacific Ocean."

Angel's voice is heard throughout the hall. "The Great Pacific Garbage Patch is one of the many **plastic gyres** within the bodies of water on our planet and is known as the Pacific trash vortex. These floating plastic debris areas are called plastic gyres because the ocean currents move in circular and gyre motions and collect all the litter that enters the ocean into condensed plastic soups. There are around 26 billion pieces of litter along U.S. waterways. 80% of all marine pollution is plastic waste. Every year, 8 to 10 million metric tons of plastic end up in the ocean. It is predicted that if litter continues at the current rate, by 2050, plastic will outweigh fish in the sea."

Jessica raises her hand and Angel picks her to speak. "You just said that this is a prediction?! Does this mean that something can change?"

Angel smiles at Jessica. "I am so glad you pointed this out. Yes, this is a prediction. If we can get people on the planet to change their habits that are causing waste to enter the oceans, things can change, and the ocean can heal. We need to get people to stop littering and to start avoiding using single-use plastic items whenever possible."

Ram points to a plastic bottle in the picture of the Pacific gyre. "We can get people to use reusable water bottles at school to help reduce the use of plastic bottles."

Angel smiles at Ram. "That's a great example of a positive change we can make. There are many problems with plastic in our environment. One of the problems is that plastic in the ocean becomes toxic. Plastic in the water attracts toxin contaminants that enter the waterways and become more toxic. Using reusables as much as possible is a way to completely avoid these harmful materials while preventing them from entering our oceans and harming marine life."

Ms. Olive, Jessica, Ram, and Joelle all clap their hands in gratitude for the tour.

Angel finishes the tour with his final words. "You have the power to make the change we need in our world."

Ms. Olive approaches Angel and shakes his hand. "Thank you so much for this experience. It was highly informative." Jessica, Joelle, and Ram nod their heads in agreement.

Joelle adds, "Yes, I think our presentation to the school will be full of powerful reasons why we must make changes at school. Thank you for your help, Angel!"

Ms. Olive takes Jessica, Ram, and Joelle back to their homes. On the drive back from the aquarium, she took the fastest route since it is getting late and she wants to get them all home in time for dinner.

When Jessica finally arrives home, she is greeted by Grandma Charlotte, who encourages her to put her belongings down in the living room and motions Jessica to the dining room. Dinner is already on the table and Grace is sitting and waiting for both of them to sit down.

Plates of spaghetti, garlic bread, and salad are at the table, which is one of Jessica's favorite dinners. Jessica goes to the kitchen to wash her hands, walks back into the dining room, and sits in front of her plate of food. Jessica takes a bite of her spaghetti since she worked up an appetite from the long day.

Grandma Charlotte and Grace patiently wait for Jessica to begin sharing her experience. Grandma Charlotte motions to the food. "I made you one of your favorite meals. I'm excited to hear about your adventure today."

Jessica finishes chewing her food and starts sharing her day-long adventure with her family. "We started with a litter pickup. It was horrifying how much litter we found by the marsh. There were so many single-use plastics. I just couldn't believe how much was in the environment right by the water, directly leading to the Bay and into the Pacific Ocean." Jessica continues to share the story and facts she learned with her friends during the litter pickup.

Grace looks at Jessica and her mother and says, "Wow, that seems like quite a morning. You also went to the Monterey Aquarium, correct?" Grace takes a bite of her garlic bread and waits for Jessica to finish swallowing before she takes another bite of her spaghetti.

"Yes, the aquarium was amazing. We learned so many important facts about how plastic impacts ocean habitats," Jessica shares enthusiastically. "Did you know that the ocean produces 50% of the world's oxygen from phytoplankton photosynthesis?"

Both Grandma Charlotte and Grace shake their heads. Grace adds, "I always assumed forests and rainforests produced most of the oxygen."

"Nope," Jessica continues. "The ocean actually holds a majority of the planet's carbon and produces a majority of the world's oxygen, and that's why it's so important that we get people to stop littering. Most land litter enters into waterways and ends up in the oceans, and the plastics are disrupting the habitats that we depend on." Jessica shares all she learned from Angel at the aquarium while Grandma Charlotte and Grace listen attentively.

COMPOST
BENEFITS
OF
COMPOSTING
AND
RECYCLING
Recycling

CHAPTER TWELVE:
Green Teams
Save the Blue Macaw, Part II

Finally, the school assembly day has arrived. Jessica, Joelle, and Ram had been preparing for many days. They are waiting in their school's multipurpose room, standing on stage behind the curtain. They have their note cards and work on a PowerPoint presentation that has slides of pictures and examples of the story they want to share with their school.

Joelle and Ram are very confident speaking in front of the school. Jessica, however, still has a fear of speaking in front of many people, especially kids her age. She still fears getting made fun of or mocked if she says something awkward or wrong. Having her two friends by her side helps calm her nerves a little, but she is still slightly shaking as she holds her note cards, and the palms of her hands are sweaty.

Joelle speaks to Ram and Jessica. "This is so exciting! I can't wait to share our presentation with everyone."

Ram replies, "Yeah, me too. I think we can get everyone to

change their habits. I mean, once we share how littering hurts turtles, why would anyone want to continue bad habits if they know they're harming wildlife?!"

Joelle and Ram look over at Jessica and notice that she looks a little uneasy. They both offer her a hug, and Joelle shares words of encouragement. "You'll be great, Jess. Plus, Ram and I will be right next to you. We're doing this together. We're a team!"

Jessica does her best to smile at her two friends and tries her best to relax.

Suddenly, the voices of other students enter the multipurpose room, and teachers can be heard giving their classes instructions on where to sit for the assembly.

Ram looks at both his friends and says with a wide smile, "It's almost showtime."

Joelle jumps up and down excitedly, and Jessica starts to panic, breathing a little harder than she had a moment before. Just then, Ms. Olive appears backstage and puts her hand on Jessica's shoulder for comfort and moral support.

Ms. Olive says in a gentle voice, "Jessica, just breathe. You will be fine. All of you will do great. Pretend you are practicing in front of only me and your families while you're up on stage. I will be in the audience cheering you on." Ms. Olive gives her three students big hugs and exits the backstage stairs leading to the audience area.

Mr. Rodgers appears backstage and greets his three students. "We're just about ready to start." The principal then goes in front of the curtain, welcomes the school, and introduces the special assembly and speakers.

The curtain opens, and Ram, Joelle, and Jessica are revealed, standing on one side of the projector screen.

Ram starts first with the team's introduction. "We're the Blue Macaw Green Team."

Joelle steps forward. "Our slogan is 'Save the Blue Macaw: reduce, reuse, recycle, and compost!'"

It's Jessica's turn to speak. She clears her throat, trying to stop her hands from shaking noticeably. "The Blue Macaw is not the only animal threatened with extinction. Hundreds of thousands of wildlife on this planet have lost their lives and habitats due to the exploitation of natural resources and waste."

Jessica looks at Ram because it's his turn to speak. "That's why we started our club at school. We want to become one of the solutions by starting a resource recovery program here at school."

Ram moves his hand, motioning for Joelle to speak next. "Ram, Jessica, and I have put a presentation together for all of you. We will share what we have learned, where natural resources come from, how resource extraction can hurt our planet, and how waste and wasteful behaviors and practices harm our planet."

The students begin to share their PowerPoint presentation slides in front of their entire school. They cover the destruction of habitats and ecosystems due to unsustainable practices and resource over-extraction. They cover how paper, plastic, metal, and glass are produced, and share about food production leading to biodiversity loss. They talk about how unsustainable practices are leading causes of climate change and how discarding resources as waste in landfills just turns resources into toxins, further harming the planet.

Jessica's turn comes up, and she shares what happens to waste when it's burned. "An alternative to landfilling is burning waste in **incinerators**: big factories that burn waste to 'get rid of it.' The incinerator creates dioxins. **Dioxins** are harmful chemicals that can travel in the air and eventually fall in the Arctic because it's cold. 80% of the dioxin levels on the planet are caused by the incineration of waste." She points to another graph called **Global Distillation**, which shows a picture of a tower-looking factory (an incinerator) releasing toxins into the air with arrows pointing to a picture of an icecap in the Arctic. "For example, global distillation is a process where toxic chemicals move through the air from warmer areas of the planet to colder climates and fall dormant."

The slide changes to show a short ten-second video of part of a glacier breaking off and falling into the Arctic. It's Joelle's turn to speak, and she points to the video. "Due to the changes in climate around the planet, the Arctic is getting warmer and ice sheets are melting, releasing the dioxins into the ocean. This is adding to the plastic crisis. The irony here is that plastic is made from fossil fuels. Fossil fuels are one of the drivers of climate change, driving glaciers in the Arctic to melt and release these dioxins into the ocean."

Still shaking slightly, Jessica steps forward and explains, "This is another example of how our waste exacerbates the planet's environmental crisis, and it's all interconnected."

Jessica looks over to Ram for him to share the next slide, which changes to a diagram showing how litter ends up in waterways through creeks, rivers, storm drains, lakes, and the ocean. Ram says with conviction, "This leads to the next part of the story, when waste is not landfilled or incinerated but becomes **land-based marine debris**. Land-based marine debris is a term for everyday trash littering. Land-based debris can include plastic bags, plastic bottles, straws, bottle caps, utensils, food containers, food wrappers, plastic lids, styrofoam, chip bags, and so much more."

Jessica steps toward the diagram and points to the street and storm drain. "Litter is swept, blown, and washed out into the ocean. For example, storm water that flows along streets can carry litter into storm drains, which can end up in lakes, rivers, and the ocean. 80% of marine litter is from land, and 85% of that is plastic."

The next slide appears, and it's Joelle's turn to speak again. There are two separate pictures on this slide: one of a fish with a predator about to eat it and another of a plate of salmon. "Remember how we mentioned dioxins created from burning waste and the glaciers melting releases the toxins into the ocean? Well, toxins, just like dioxins, attach to plastic in the ocean like magnets, making the plastics more toxic. Many studies and research show that most marine life is eating plastics. The toxic plastics end up in the food chain and can even end up on our plates."

The slide changes to a map of all the bodies of water and the currents on the planet. Jessica points to the map and says, "Plastics in the ocean are being discovered and look like large, condensed, plastic-like soups, some twice the size of Texas, and they are called plastic gyres. These are the gyres: the North Pacific Gyre, South Pacific Gyre, North Atlantic Gyre, South Atlantic Gyre, and Indian Ocean Gyre. An estimated 50-70 trillion pieces of plastic and microplastics are in the ocean."

The slide changes once again, revealing in a big bold font: "Solutions: Save the Blue Macaw." Joelle starts to share with the school what they learned during the waste audit on campus. "50% of our school's waste is compostable. If our school's compost and biodegradables go to the landfill, then we are contributing to methane gas emissions, which contribute to climate change. Climate change impacts natural habitats of **endangered species**, like the blue macaw, changing their ecosystems and food supply."

The slide now shows a picture of the blue macaw in the Amazon rainforest. Ram continues to share: "The blue macaw is in danger due to deforestation. Some of the causes of deforestation are land clearing for agriculture, food, and resources like paper." Jessica holds up some cleaned examples from their waste audit showing the school an empty milk carton, juice box, and a cardboard lunch box. Ram points to what Jessica is holding and explains, "These three items are just examples of the hundreds and hundreds of milk cartons, juice boxes, cardboard boxes, and paper thrown away at school daily, weekly, and yearly. At our school, 30% of the waste is paper, like reading and writing paper and paper towels. Suppose we don't recycle paper or compost it. In that case, we participate in the demands that cause more trees to be cut down, contributing to the loss of ecosystems and habitats and driving extinction to the blue macaws and other wildlife on the planet."

Jessica holds up two more examples of items they found in the waste audit: an empty soda can and a plastic water bottle. Joelle points to both objects in her friend's hands and shares, "Throwing away metals and plastics drives the demand to drill and mine for natural resources, which leads to destroying habitats. Not to mention that every time someone litters on campus or doesn't pick up after themselves, they are contributing to the gyres and harmful toxic waste that are taking over our oceans and land."

Jessica puts down the soda can and plastic water bottle and motions to the next slide that shows a green compost bin, blue recycle bin, and gray landfill bin. "Our solution is to start sorting our waste during lunch, in the classrooms, bathrooms, and on the blacktop outside. We need your help to be successful. We need everyone to join us on our mission to stop the waste at school. You can do this by composting any leftover food scraps, food-soiled paper, paper towels, and paper napkins. We need you to recycle all the reading and writing paper in the classrooms, your empty milk cartons, juice boxes, and plastic containers like applesauce cups and yogurt cups, and to recycle any metal cans, aluminum foil, and glass bottles."

Joelle holds up her reusable water bottle, her lunchbox full of reusable containers, and her reusable fork, spoon, and napkin. "We also encourage everyone to use reusables whenever you can. Reusing helps us stop waste at the source."

Jessica stands next to Joelle and continues with her last statement. "Reducing our school waste by recycling and composting will help us lower our environmental footprint. Please help our school be part of the bigger picture that goes beyond our community, so our efforts will help save the lives of blue macaws and other species on this planet."

Ram stands next to Jessica and finishes with a big smile. "Help our school reduce its waste; help us save the blue macaw."

Ram, Jessica, and Joelle bow to the audience and say "thank you" in unison. The multipurpose room erupts in cheers.

CHAPTER THIRTEEN

The Great Return to Grandma's Secret Garden

After a successful assembly, Ms. Olive, Mr. Green, Mr. Rodgers, Jessica, Joelle, and Ram work together and set up the changes around the school so that everyone can start recycling and composting. Jessica's personality begins to blossom as she learns the valuable lesson that she, with the support of her friends, can make a difference within their community. Feeling very accomplished by the end of the school week, on Friday after school, Jessica invites Joelle and Ram over for dinner to celebrate their victory.

They walk together to Jessica's house after school, charged with positive energy from the eventful week at school.

Joelle looks at her friends, delighted. "Can you believe how much of a difference we made this week?!"

Ram responds enthusiastically, "I know, right? We are helping our school become one of the first schools in the district to become sustainable."

Jessica beams with a bright smile. "It all started with our investigation into waste. Actually, it started when we all decided to become friends."

Joelle moves closer to Jessica to hug her as they walk. "I am glad we became friends. It's been inspiring."

Just then, Jessica's mind wanders to the friends she left behind, her special friends in Grandma's Secret Garden. Jessica, walking in the middle, looks over at both Ram and Joelle next to her. "You know what?" Joelle and Ram look at Jessica with curiosity, not knowing what she will share. Jessica continues, "You both are my first real friends. I was too afraid to talk to other kids for a long time. But I have special friends who are not human and are in my grandmother's garden. Can I introduce you both to them?"

Joelle and Ram look past Jessica over at each other and then back at Jessica, smiling at her in agreement.

Joelle says with curiosity, "This sounds very interesting."

Once they arrive at Jessica's house and enter the front door, Bear, the family dog, greets them. Bear jumps off the couch and rushes to Jessica to give her his big smile. Jessica picks him up, and he gives her a lick on her cheek. She giggles with joy, putting down her furry friend. "Hi, Bear. Joelle and Ram came home with me today."

Joelle and Ram kneel on the carpeted living room floor and pet the happy little dog as he wiggles his body back and forth between their loving petting hands.

The kitchen releases a yummy aroma of tomatoes, basil, garlic, and other spices into the living room.

Jessica proudly explains, "Grandma Charlotte agreed to make us lasagna using the squash she has grown in the garden. Speaking of the garden, let's go meet my special friends."

All three place their backpacks down neatly by the front door and start heading to the back of the house.

Grandma Charlotte greets them as they enter the kitchen and walk toward the back door. All three of them greet Grandma Charlotte with a smile and a hello.

Grandma Charlotte stops cutting garlic by the kitchen counter and looks over her shoulder at the children passing by. "Well, hello, kids. Dinner will be done in about an hour. Are you all hungry? Would you like a snack?"

Jessica greets her grandmother with a huge hug. "I think I can wait for dinner. How about you, Joelle, or you, Ram? Would you like a snack?"

Both Joelle and Ram respond politely, "No, thank you."

Grandma Charlotte smiles at them. "Okay, well, dinner will be ready soon enough." She then goes back to work on preparing dinner.

Jessica leads her friends to the back door, and Bear follows happily behind them. Bear finds a sunny spot by the flowers and lies down, enjoying the last of the sun's rays. As they enter Grandma's Secret Garden, Joelle and Ram are welcomed with the soft smells of flowers blooming as a bumblebee and butterfly visit the flowers. They see the apple tree, the giant oak tree with the treehouse, and the hummingbird fluttering nearby. They notice a squirrel scurry out of the treehouse and sit on the oak tree's branch, observing them from above. Jessica walks them to the fairy bench and motions for them to sit. "Well, my friends, here they are."

Joelle and Ram look at each other and then Jessica, confused. Joelle is the first to speak. "Who?"

Jessica says delightedly, pointing to the ground near the birdbath, "There's Mr. and Mrs. Wiggles."

"Well, hello, Res. The Mrs. and I have not seen you in quite some time." Mr. Wiggles greets his friend.

Mrs. Wiggles responds with interest, "I see you brought friends."

Jessica motions to Joelle and Ram. "Yes, these are my new friends from school. I have been spending a lot of time with them, which is why you haven't seen me lately."

Joelle and Ram sit on the fairy bench, watching their friend talk to earthworms on the ground. They don't know how to react and try their best to hide their shock and concern for their friend. They think she's lost her mind.

"And this is Beau and Bumbles." Jessica giggles as the butterfly flutters by her nose. The honeybee buzzes, traveling slightly toward the fairy bench.

"Yes, it's been so long. How are you?" Sunny the Squirrel leaps from the oak tree's branches to Terry's branch.

"Yes, we've missed you," Terry joins in with the friendly greetings.

Ram and Joelle sit speechless as they observe Jessica talking to her grandmother's garden inhabitants, appearing to have a conversation with herself.

They see Jessica waving her arms in delight as she looks at the squirrel, insects, trees, and hummingbird. "Oh, I miss you all too—so much. I want you to meet my friends from school, Joelle and Ram." Jessica turns to her two friends sitting on the fairy bench very still, with looks of concern on their faces.

Jessica's smile disappears and is replaced with dread. "You don't believe me." There is an awkward silence. Jessica's shoulders slump forward, and she sits near Terry the Apple Tree's trunk. She looks up to her two friends sitting on the bench. "Are you able to hear them?"

Joelle and Ram look at each other as if trying to figure out how to respond to Jessica's question without hurting her feelings. They turn their heads back to Jessica and shake their heads. "No."

Jessica's eyes start to well up, and she does her best to hold back tears of sadness and embarrassment.

Flora zooms at Jessica's face. "Res, don't cry. They may not be able to hear us, but you can. Maybe you can bridge the communication."

All the special friends say, "Yes," in agreement.

"But how?" Jessica says in despair.

Ram scoots over to Joelle on the bench and whispers to his friend. "This is a little weird. What should we do?"

Joelle looks at Ram and is about to whisper back when the hummingbird zooms in front of them.

Startled and surprised, both Joelle and Ram sit straight up, looking at the bird hovering in front of them. Jessica approaches them slowly and points to the bird. "This is my friend, Flora. She's going to help me communicate so that you can hear them speak through me and trust that what I am saying is true. Flora is going to land on your hand, Joelle. Don't be scared, and don't move."

Just then, the hummingbird did just that. It hovered by Joelle's folded hands in her lap and landed on her hand. The hummingbird looked up at Joelle. Joelle locked eyes with the little bird and felt a thrilling rush of pure amazement.

Jessica speaks again. "Ram, Sunny the Squirrel is going to help me too. Sunny wants to sit on your shoulder. Please, don't be afraid; just relax and sit still."

Sure enough, Ram watches the squirrel scurry down from the

apple tree and run over to the fairy bench. The squirrel climbs up his jeans and shirt and sits on his shoulder.

Both Ram and Joelle sit on the fairy bench, speechless and in awe, as they observe the wildlife in the backyard respond to them and to Jessica. Grandma's Secret Garden is silent for a while. Jessica stands in front of her friends with a butterfly and bee perched on both her hands. Finally, Jessica breaks the silence. "Now do you believe me?"

Joelle and Ram look at their friend with amazement and quietly say, "Yes." Flora flies toward Jessica; Sunny leaps off Ram's shoulder and runs back to Terry the Apple Tree's branches; and Beau and Bumbles flutter and buzz back to the flowers. The garden erupts in cheers that only Jessica can hear.

CHAPTER FOURTEEN:
Soil is a Network

Jessica sits under Terry the Apple Tree's branches and shares stories back and forth between her special nature friends and Joelle and Ram. Jessica shares the adventures she and her friends at school had in setting up the brand-new recycling and compost program. She also explains what they learned during the litter pickup and about plastic pollution.

"That sounds awful, all the plastic hurting the ocean. There must be something humans can do to fix this," Terry responds to hearing about the plastic pollution crisis.

Jessica looks over to Ram and Joelle, telling them what Terry said.

Ram responds, shaking his head, "I wish there were a solution. Six hundred billion PET water bottles are made yearly. People need to stop using plastics."

Joelle adds, "Please tell Terry our solution is to slow down and reduce the use of plastics at school with our reusables during lunch and zero-waste campaign."

Jessica smiles at her friends and begins to explain the plan to the special friends, who are all gathered near Terry the Apple Tree, listening.

Anna Mycelium speaks up. "Hi friends; I have actually been receiving information from the underground mycelium network. Some of the other fungi are able to break down plastics."

Jessica's eyes grow wide with excitement as she hears this news. "Wow, this is amazing! You have to tell me more." Jessica motions towards Anna Mycelium, visible near the oak tree's trunk.

Joelle and Ram want to know what the excitement is about. Joelle inquires, "What's happening now? Who are you talking to?"

Jessica points to the mushroom with the red umbrella-like top and white dots. "This is Anna Mycelium. Apparently, Anna Mycelium just received information from her underground communication channels that there are fungi that can break down plastic."

Ram looks at Anna Mycelium and says, "You have our full attention. We have to hear about this."

Jessica speaks to Anna Mycelium, encouraging her to continue sharing the new information.

Anna Mycelium begins to speak to all the friends in the garden. "Res, do you remember our last conversation about ecosystems? I explained that I am a fungus and that fungi are known as decomposers. Fungi's responsibility as decomposers is to break down the material and return its nutrients to the earth, using the ground's mycelium, our thread root system. Well, apparently, some specific fungi can use their mycelium root system to break down plastics."

Jessica is so excited to share what she just heard with Joelle and Ram. "Apparently, there are fungi that can use their root systems to break down plastics. So there are solutions to return plastic to nature without waiting hundreds of years for it to break down!"

Ram and Joelle look at Jessica with astonishment. Ram asks, "Is it possible for some of these fungi to be used in the ocean to help break down the plastic pollution there, too?"

Jessica looks back at Anna Mycelium and tells her of Ram's concern for the ocean.

Anna responds with delight and begins to share all the information being shared through the mycelium network. "Why, yes, absolutely! There is a fungus that lives in the ocean called the Parengyodontium album, and it works with other microbes to break down plastic. Apparently, it can break down polyethylene. The plastic needs to be exposed to sunlight first, but after that happens, the fungi can break it down."

Jessica shares the information she just learned with her two attentive friends. "Apparently, mushrooms are the Earth's recyclers, and their way is healthier for the planet. They are actually a part of nature's biomass recycling program. Not only that, but some mushrooms, like the oyster mushroom, clean up plastics and toxins, too."

Joelle can't hold back her excitement. "They're the best recyclers because they leave the Earth better than they found it. Humanity needs to learn from nature. The solutions are everywhere, even in places we may not see or that we take for granted."

"This is great!" Ram shouts with excitement. "Mushrooms and healthy soil do so much for our planet. Now I am excited about our school helping turn our food scraps into compost."

Jessica explains to her special friends in the garden what they have learned about food waste and how their school's green team is helping reduce greenhouse gasses by composting.

Anna Mycelium is happy to hear this news. "Wow, you children are doing so much great work! You and your friends may also be glad to hear that when the mycelium breaks materials down, it creates nutrient-dense soil that reduces erosion. This soil also helps plants grow by underground networks called mycorrhizal networks that transfer nutrients like nitrogen and carbon."

Terry the Apple Tree joins the conversation. "Yes, we trees use the **mycorrhizal network** to talk to each other, and we can send nutrients from stronger plants to help the weaker ones! This network allows us to stay connected and help each other grow, live, and thrive." Terry's branches gently sway in the light breeze toward Ram and Joelle. "Res, your friends look like they want to know more about what we just shared."

Jessica agrees and turns her attention back to her two friends, who are now smiling from ear to ear at the news they are learning in Grandma's Secret Garden. Jessica finishes with her last words. "Well, my dear friends, everything seems to truly be connected. Everything in nature is connected."

The gentle breeze picks up, and the leaves begin to rustle on the ground.
Grandma Charlotte's voice can be heard from the kitchen. "Children, dinner is ready. Bear, come back inside; your dinner is ready, too."

Bear, who had fallen fast asleep, wakes up and runs toward Charlotte's voice at the back door leading inside the house.

Jessica, Ram, and Joelle stand up and look at Grandma's Secret Garden, with all their friends looking back at them. Jessica waves goodbye, saying goodnight, and Joelle and Ram follow her lead. All three of them walk toward the house with enthusiasm for the future, because they are now empowered with real solutions and hope for the planet.

Everyday Challenge:
Make a Difference Today

1. Become a Zero-Waste Hero:

- **Challenge:** Can you reduce how much trash you make in one week? Try using a reusable water bottle, lunchbox, and snack bags. See if you can avoid single-use plastic for an entire week!
- **Tip:** Create a zero-waste kit with your family, including items like reusable bags, bamboo utensils, and stainless-steel straws.

2. Start Your Own Green Garden:

- **Challenge:** Grow your own mini garden with seeds, soil, and a small pot. You can grow herbs, flowers, or even veggies like lettuce or tomatoes!
- **Tip:** Compost leftover fruit and veggie scraps to help your plants grow. It's fun to watch nature's cycle in action!

131

3. Be a Fungi Detective:

   • **Challenge:** Explore your local park or garden to see if you can spot any mushrooms or fungi growing. Remember, they're nature's recyclers!
   • **Tip:** Take pictures of the different mushrooms you find and research what type they are. You might find one that's helping the trees around it grow!

4. Clean Up Your Neighborhood:

   • **Challenge:** Organize a cleanup day with your   friends and family. Pick up litter in your park, beach, or around your school to keep your local area clean and healthy.
   • **Tip:** Bring gloves and a trash bag, and make a game out of who can collect the most litter. Every little bit helps!

5. Become a Nature Protector:

   • **Challenge:** Learn about one animal or plant that is in danger from pollution or climate change. Share what you've learned with your class or family, and explain why it's important to protect them.
   • **Tip:** Create a poster or story about your chosen animal or plant to spread awareness.

6. Save Water and Energy:

   • **Challenge:** Try turning off the water while brushing your teeth, or see if you can shorten your shower by two minutes.
   • **Tip:** Unplug chargers and electronics when you're not using them. It saves energy and helps the planet!

7. Make Your Own Art from Recycled Materials:

- **Challenge:** Use things like old newspapers, bottle caps, or cardboard to make a cool art project. You're turning trash into treasure!
- **Tip:** Have an art contest with your friends to see who can create the most creative artwork using only recycled materials.

8. Learn About Mushrooms that Can Eat Plastic!

- **Challenge:** Research more about how fungi like oyster mushrooms can break down plastics. Maybe one day, you'll be a scientist who discovers new ways to fight pollution!
- **Tip:** Start a mushroom-growing kit at home to see how fungi grow and help the environment.

9. Write a Letter to Your School:

- **Challenge:** Ask your school to go green! Write a letter to your principal with ideas like starting a school recycling program or adding more plants to your classroom.
- **Tip:** Get your classmates involved. Together, you can make a big difference!

10. Spread the Word:

- **Challenge:** Share what you've learned about plastic pollution, climate change, and fungi with a friend or family member. The more people who know, the bigger the impact!

- **Tip:** Host a "green day," where everyone learns one new thing they can do to help the environment.

Join the Resilience Earth Warrior Family!

Get ready to be a true Earth Warrior! Join our Resilience Earth Warrior Family by signing up for the **Earth Warrior Carbon Calculator.** It's a fun and easy way to track your daily sustainable actions, like walking, carpooling, composting, recycling, and reusing.

With your Earth Warrior account, you'll be able to see how your actions help fight climate change by saving trees, reducing waste, and even being equivalent to removing cars from the road—just by doing simple things every day!

The Earth Warrior Carbon Calculator is your guide to achieving Zero Waste and making a big impact! You'll learn how to make a difference from:

- **Waste Reduction 101:**
    Start by recycling and composting.

- **Waste Reduction 201:**
    Reuse what you can and say no to unnecessary items!

- **Waste Reduction 301:**
    Try a Veggie Challenge Day!

Join the fun by trying a Veggie Challenge Day, where you go without dairy or meat for just one day a week. It's a simple way to explore plant-based foods and see how it helps the planet!

Even small changes, like adding more fruits and veggies, can make a big difference. And if your family raises cows or other animals, you can still be part of the challenge by finding other fun ways to reduce waste!

- **Sustainable Miles Traveled:**
    Track your trips, whether you're walking, biking, or carpooling.

Each action you take helps protect our planet, and you'll see how much carbon you're keeping out of the atmosphere.

Together, we can reach 9 of the **17 United Nations Sustainable Development Goals**—and every small action counts!

Become an Earth Warrior today and let's change the world!

Sign up for your free account today at **www.RBRORG.org**.

Works Cited

Action Metals Recyclers. "What Are the Environmental Impacts of Metals in a Landfill?" Action Metals Recyclers, www.action-metalsrecyclers.com/what-are-the-environmental-impacts-of-metals-in-a-landfill/. Accessed May 2024.

Better Place Forests. "Mycelium and Mycorrhizal in the Forest." Better Place Forests, www.betterplaceforests.com/blog/mycelium-and-mycorrhizal-in-the-forest/. Accessed May 2024.

Biological Diversity. "Mountaintop Removal Mining." Center for Biological Diversity, www.biologicaldiversity.org/programs/public_lands/mining/mountaintop_removal/. Accessed May 2024.

Clean Water Action. "Marine Plastic Pollution." Clean Water Action, cleanwater.org/problem-marine-plastic-pollution. Accessed May 2024.

Colorado Environmental Center. "Hidden Damage of Landfills." University of Colorado Boulder, 15 Apr. 2021, www.colorado.edu/ecenter/2021/04/15/hidden-damage-landfills. Accessed May 2024.

Colorado Environmental Center. "Plastic-Eating Mushrooms: A Viable Solution?" University of Colorado Boulder, 4 Nov. 2021, www.colorado.edu/ecenter/2021/11/04/plastic-eating-mushrooms-viable-solution-plastic-decomposition. Accessed May 2024.

Earth.org. "Amazon Rainforest Deforestation Facts." Earth.org, earth.org/amazon-rainforest-deforestation-facts/. Accessed May 2024.

Environmental Protection Agency. "National Overview: Facts and Figures on Materials, Waste and Recycling." EPA, www.epa.gov/facts-and-figures-about-materials-waste-and-recycling/national-overview-facts-and-figures-materials. Accessed May 2024.

European Environment Agency. European Marine Litter Assessment. EEA, www.eea.europa.eu/publications/european-marine-litter-assessment. Accessed May 2024.

Fantastic Fungi. "10 Things to Know About the Mycelial Network." Fantastic Fungi, fantasticfungi.com/blogs/news/10-things-to-know-about-the-mycelial-network. Accessed May 2024.

Geoterra Dominicana. "The Environmental Impact of Silica Sand Extraction and Sustainable Solutions." Geoterra Dominicana, www.geoterradominicana.com/en/articles/the-environmental-impact-of-silica-sand-extraction-and-sustainable-solutions/. Accessed May 2024.

Green Earth. "Top 10 Causes of Deforestation." Green.earth, www.green.earth/blog/top-10-causes-of-deforestation. Accessed May 2024.

Intergovernmental Panel on Climate Change. Climate Change 2023: Synthesis Report. IPCC, 2023, www.ipcc.ch/report/ar6/syr/. Accessed May 2024.

Keep America Beautiful. "End Litter." Keep America Beautiful, kab.org/litter/end-litter/. Accessed May 2024.

LRL Minnesota. "Industrial Silica Sand (Frac Sand)." Minnesota Legislature Reference Library, www.lrl.mn.gov/guides/guides?issue=fracsands. Accessed May 2024.

Marine Debris Program. "Ingestion." National Oceanic and Atmospheric Administration, marinedebris.noaa.gov/why-marine-debris-problem/ingestion. Accessed May 2024.

Marine Debris Program. "Land-Based Marine Debris." National Oceanic and Atmospheric Administration, marinedebris.noaa.gov/where-does-marine-debris-come/land-based-marine-debris. Accessed May 2024.

Massachusetts Environmental Services. "6 Scary Paper Waste Facts." MES Ltd., blog.mesltd.ca/6-scary-paper-waste-facts. Accessed May 2024.

MIT Climate Portal. "Soil-Based Carbon Sequestration." MIT Climate, climate.mit.edu/explainers/soil-based-carbon-sequestration. Accessed May 2024.

National Academies of Sciences, Engineering, and Medicine. The Challenge of Feeding the World Sustainably: Summary of the US-UK Scientific Forum on Sustainable Agriculture. National Academies Press, 2021, doi:10.17226/26007.

National Geographic Society. "Great Pacific Garbage Patch." National Geographic Education, education.nationalgeographic.org/resource/great-pacific-garbage-patch/. Accessed May

2024.

National Oceanic and Atmospheric Administration. "Microplastics." NOAA Ocean Service, oceanservice.noaa.gov/facts/microplastics.html. Accessed May 2024.

Paperonweb. "How Much Paper Is Consumed per Year?" Paperonweb, www.paperonweb.com/A1006.htm. Accessed May 2024.

Recycle Cartons. Carton Council Start-Up Guide 2024. Carton Council of North America, 2024, recyclecartons.com/wp-content/uploads/2024/04/CC_StartUpGuide-2024.pdf.

Rubicon. "Effects of Mismanaged Trash on Wildlife." Rubicon, www.rubicon.com/blog/effects-mismanaged-trash-on-wildlife/. Accessed May 2024.

ScienceDaily. "New Advances in Plastic Decomposition." ScienceDaily, 3 June 2024, www.sciencedaily.com/releases/2024/06/240603114314.htm. Accessed May 2024.

Stanford News. "One of Earth's Biggest Carbon Sinks May Be Overestimated." Stanford University, 2021, news.stanford.edu/stories/2021/03/one-earths-biggest-carbon-sinks-overestimated. Accessed May 2024.

Stockton Recycles. "Top 10 Littered Items." Stockton Recycles, stocktonrecycles.com/top-10-littered-items/. Accessed May 2024.

UNESCO. "Plastic Pollution and the Ocean." Ocean Literacy Portal, oceanliteracy.unesco.org/plastic-pollution-ocean/.

Accessed May 2024.

United Nations. "Biodiversity and Climate Change." United Nations Climate Action, www.un.org/en/climatechange/science/climate-issues/biodiversity. Accessed May 2024.

United Nations. "What Is Plastic Pollution?" United Nations Sustainable Development, Aug. 2023, www.un.org/sustainabledevelopment/blog/2023/08/explainer-what-is-plastic-pollution/. Accessed May 2024.

Visual Capitalist. "All the Metals We Mined in 2021, Visualized." Visual Capitalist, www.visualcapitalist.com/all-the-metals-we-mined-in-2021-visualized/. Accessed May 2024.

World Wildlife Fund. "Whales and the Plastics Problem." WWF, www.worldwildlife.org/stories/whales-and-the-plastics-problem. Accessed May 2024.

Zurich Insurance Group. "Food for Thought: What Biodiversity Means to You." Zurich Magazine, www.zurich.com/en/media/magazine/2021/food-for-thought-what-biodiversity-means-to-you. Accessed May 2024.